"In *Pulpy & Midge*, you end up genuinely liking the title characters, not just as characters, but as people ... Westhead has a real gift for dialogue, creating a vibrant world that exists almost completely between quotation marks ... Because almost everyone in *Pulpy & Midge* is polite, the tension inhabits the spaces between the lines, cold as ice."

— BROKEN PENCIL

"Don't let the cartoonish title fool you — the book's most obvious comparison is the TV series *The Office*; *Pulpy & Midge* has the same wry pacing. With charming design and a storyteller's skill, Westhead keeps her fiction fresh by letting the audience follow the characters through ordinary workdays as Pulpy waits for his imminent promotion."

— EYE WEEKLY

and also
sharks

and also sharks

stories by

jessica westhead

Cormorant Books

Canada Council   Conseil des Arts
for the Arts   du Canada

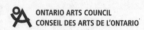 ONTARIO ARTS COUNCIL
CONSEIL DES ARTS DE L'ONTARIO

 Canadian   Patrimoine   Canadä
Heritage   canadien

The publisher gratefully acknowledges the support of the Canada Council for the Arts
and the Ontario Arts Council for its publishing program. We acknowledge the
financial support of the Government of Canada through the Canada Book Fund (CBF)
for our publishing activities, and the Government of Ontario through the Ontario
Media Development Corporation, an agency of the Ontario Ministry of Culture, and
the Ontario Book Publishing Tax Credit Program.

Library and Archives Canada Cataloguing in Publication

Westhead, Jessica, 1974-
And also sharks / Jessica Westhead.

Short stories.
ISBN 978-1-77086-003-2

1. Title.

PS8645.E85A54 2011   C813'.6   C2010-907929-9

Cover art: Lindsay Page
Cover design: Angel Guerra/Archetype
Interior text design: Tannice Goddard, Soul Oasis Networking
Printer: Marquis

Printed and bound in Canada.

This book is printed on 100% post-consumer waste recycled paper.

CORMORANT BOOKS INC.
215 SPADINA AVENUE, STUDIO 230, TORONTO, ONTARIO, CANADA M5T 2C7
www.cormorantbooks.com

RECYCLED
Paper made from
recycled material
FSC® C021757

For my parents, Linda and Tim Westhead.
With love and thanks, for everything.

Contents

and also
sharks

We Are All
About Wendy Now

OUR OFFICE IS VERY community-minded. We hold two food drives a year: the first one at Thanksgiving and the second one not at Christmas, because the poor people get so much food from other food drives at Christmas that we like to surprise them with something extra on a random day when they're not expecting it.

We also look out for, as Sherry puts it, "our own little community." People are always asking how everybody is, how everybody's family is. Personally, I have never had much time for socializing at work. My reports keep me busy all day, right up until five o'clock when I would go home to Johnny.

Every so often, Sherry would come by my desk, sometimes after one of her vacations, and ask me how my day was going. That was about the extent of my socializing. I couldn't even tell you how many places Sherry's been; I know she's been to China and Australia, and when you go that far away you have to go for at least three weeks because of the jet lag. I only know that from

Sherry. The farthest I've ever been was to Florida with my family, and it wasn't even all that warm when we went.

"That Wendy's not right," is what Sherry said to me when she came by my desk that October noon hour, and I honestly had to think for a minute before I could picture who she meant.

"Wendy who?" I was eating my ham sandwich, and the polar ice caps were on my computer screen. Apparently they're starting to melt, if you can believe that. I gazed at that big stretch of white and I thought, *Winter is coming.* Then my wheat field scene came on, with the environmentally friendly windmills, and I felt reassured.

"Wendy, who sits next to me!" said Sherry. "Haven't you seen her lately? She looks awful, and she smells awful because she's throwing up all the time. I think she's sick with something."

Now, the way our office is set up is, there's my desk, and next to me is Val, and then across from Val is Ruth P., and then beside her is Twyla (she's a temp), and diagonal from her is Ruth C. And then there's Kevin (the only man on staff other than Mr. Vanderhoeven) next to Ruth C., and kitty-corner from them is Sherry, and then Wendy's desk was beside hers.

I knew I'd passed Wendy's desk a hundred times, because she was directly across from Mr. Vanderhoeven's office and that's who I bring my reports to every week. But at that moment, I just couldn't picture her.

"She's got streaks in her hair," said Sherry.

And then there she was, *pop*, right in my brain. Wendy with the streaks. I heard people saying a few things after she'd gotten them done. Not mean things, just sort of observations that it wasn't one of the best streak jobs they'd ever seen.

"Okay," I said. "Wendy." And right then, my Johnny screen-saver came on. I had an old photo of him in my cycle, and it always made my heart skip a beat to see him like that, from back in our early days.

"Val said she heard her throwing up in the washroom today. And I heard her in there twice yesterday."

I put down my sandwich. "Why doesn't she stay home if she's not feeling well?"

This is what I used to think about Sherry — wait, that's not what I meant to say. I never really thought anything about Sherry. Except that she always seemed like a nice person. I don't know if I would've said before all this that she was nice enough to give you the shirt off her back, but when you stop and think about it, that's a lot to ask from someone.

"She doesn't have anybody at home." Sherry's voice got lower, but somehow louder at the same time. "Her husband left her. And believe me, it was not an amicable split like me and Dave had. And they never even had any kids, isn't that tragic?" Sherry leaned in. She was wearing one of her designer suits, and up close I could see my face in one of the silver buttons. They were that shiny. "She keeps coming to work because we're all she has."

I blinked at my reflection. I looked so small there on her big, checkered lapel. "I can't understand people who don't have a life outside the office," I said.

"Oh, I know," said Sherry.

Sherry is the type of person who will make friends with her co-workers, just like that. And she does nice things for her friends, because she cares about them. Once in a blue moon I might hear other people in the office say, "Sherry's this," or

"Sherry's that," but that's only once in a blue moon, like I said.

Now, she's got a few degrees, I know that much. And she does art in her spare time. And she's divorced. And she doesn't have any pets. And she's always been nice to me. But until this whole thing with Wendy — well, all I'm saying now is this: Sherry would not only give you the shirt off her back, she would go and buy a shirt and give it to you. And even if it was the wrong size or you didn't like the style, you'd wear it, because of all the trouble she'd gone to. That's the kind of person Sherry is.

"I'm telling you, Eunice, I'm getting seriously worried about Wendy's health. There's the throwing up, and she's also tired all the time and has terrible headaches ... I even said to her last week, 'Wendy, you are unwell, and you should be home in bed.' And Wendy said, 'I'm fine, Sherry.' And I said, 'You're not.' And she said, 'Sherry, I'm fine.' But she isn't fine, Eunice, I know it." She looked at my food. "Ooh, what's that you've got there?"

"It's just a sandwich," I said.

"Ham and cheese?"

"Just ham."

"Yum." Sherry smiled at me. "How's your day going, Eunice?"

"Oh, fine."

"Did you put your cans in the Hope Horn yet?"

"Not yet, but I will." It was Sherry's idea to use a big wicker cornucopia for our Thanksgiving food drive — she told Mr. Vanderhoeven that even the disadvantaged deserve a nice presentation. "Thanks for the reminder," I said.

"Well, you know me!" Sherry nodded in the direction of the cafeteria and then gave me a little wave before continuing on her way there. "Enjoy your lunch!"

And I did, because that's the way Sherry is. She makes ordinary things feel special.

ON MY WAY HOME that day, I walked past a park where a bunch of people were playing with their dogs. They all seemed to be having a lot of fun. Throwing sticks, throwing balls. Catching the sticks and balls. But I couldn't relate. Dogs intimidate me, and I'm not afraid to say it. There is no common decency as far as a dog is concerned. I've even heard from dog owners that their dogs will eat their own business. That's right — they'll do their business, and then they'll turn around and eat it!

When I got home, the smell hit me right away and I thought, *Oh, my poor Johnny.* There is something about the smell of a cat's vomit. It breaks your heart.

Johnny had even tried to be dignified about it — the vomit was in the kitchen, and he was in the living room. But he'd gotten it on his paws and tracked it through the apartment, and I could tell he felt terrible about that. He felt bad enough when he couldn't make it to the litter box anymore, and now this.

I told him not to worry. I cleaned his paws and put him on my lap, and we watched our shows, and I petted him until he purred. His purrs weren't what they used to be, but it still made me glad to hear them.

AFTER SHERRY GOT ON board, it wasn't long before other people in the office started getting interested in how Wendy was doing, because Sherry is the type of person who makes other people want to get involved.

"How's Wendy doing?" I'd hear people asking Sherry if

Wendy wasn't at her desk when I'd go to deliver my reports.

And then about a week later, Sherry came by my desk to give me the latest Wendy update, which was that Wendy had finally taken her advice and asked for some time off work. "Isn't that wonderful?" she said.

"Sherry," I said to her (covering my mouth because I was in the middle of my ham sandwich), "you are a good friend."

"Oh, I don't know about that." Sherry wiggled her imitation Chinese take-out box in the air, which is what she uses when she brings her lunch from home (a tip she picked up in China, she told me). "I'm only doing what anybody would do. Besides, it was getting so nobody wanted to use the washroom anymore, in case Wendy was throwing up in there. We were starting to threaten Kevin that we'd take over the men's, and he'd have to wait in line like the rest of us. And do you know what he said? He said, 'Go right ahead, ladies. Mr. Vanderhoeven spends more time in there than I do.'" She giggled. "Can you believe he said that?"

The cottage vista was on my computer screen then, and I stared down someone's long dock with the calm lake and the majestic pines at the end of it. The oranges were going to come on next. I'd found a photo of a grove of them in Florida — row upon row of bright orange balls, like little suns growing on trees.

"And I'll tell you another thing. When she left, I said to her, 'Wendy, I am going to call you at home every day and make sure you're all right.'" Sherry pinched one of the many neck ruffles on her blouse and pretended to fan herself with it. "Whew, I am famished. Enjoy your sandwich, Eunice!" And she was gone.

Then you have someone like me. I don't have a home phone number for anybody at work.

FOR THE NEXT FEW weeks, Sherry came by on her way to lunch to give me the latest on how Wendy was doing — "She's sleeping better," or "She threw up six times today, can you believe that?" You could depend on Sherry to have her finger on it.

At the end of each day, I'd go home to Johnny, and we'd sit and watch our shows together, and every so often I'd notice he was a bit lighter than before. I remembered when he used to be big and round and I'd tried to put him on a diet a few times. "To make you svelte," I used to tell him, but it never worked because he enjoyed his food too much. I petted him and felt his ribs poking me and said, "You're a svelte kitty now, Johnny. What a handsome, svelte kitty you are."

ABOUT A MONTH LATER, Sherry came by my desk looking very emotional, and I could tell right away something big had happened because Sherry gets emotional when it comes to her friends.

"Eunice, you can't imagine what I've been through. Yesterday I realized Wendy's been off for a month — an entire month, Eunice. I called her up and said, 'This is ridiculous. A person does not miss a whole month of work without something being seriously wrong.' I said, 'Wendy, you are unwell, and we need to get you to a doctor. And if it means me driving you to the emergency room and waiting with you until you are seen, then so be it. So that's what I did." Sherry gasped suddenly at my computer screen. "Oh God, look at those palm trees. What I wouldn't give to be there right now, sipping rum punch with the sand between my toes. Right, Eunice? You know what I'm talking about."

I didn't, but I stared at my tropical getaway screensaver and tried to imagine the real thing.

Sherry told me she drove to Wendy's apartment, and Wendy looked about as bad as she'd ever seen her. She was all curled up on her couch in a filthy stained nightgown, and her apartment "looked like a garbage bomb had hit it."

"Not that Wendy was any sort of neat freak before all this," said Sherry. "Her desk was always a mess of papers and coffee cups and what have you."

Then she helped Wendy up and got her outside and into her car, and they went to the hospital and sat in the emergency room for hours and hours until they were seen, and then the doctor asked Wendy to describe her symptoms, and then she was sent to get a scan done, and afterwards the doctor sat them down and told Wendy she had a mass on her brain.

"Was it a CAT scan?" I said. I knew the terminology because Johnny had gotten the same thing done a few months back, and the nurse had tried to cheer me up by saying, "A CAT scan — for a cat! It's kind of funny, isn't it?" And I looked at her and said, "No, it's not funny at all." I know she meant well, but really. People forget to think sometimes.

"Yes, a CAT scan, that's it." Sherry leaned forward. "The doctor said it might be cancer. They can't confirm the diagnosis until they do a biopsy, but it doesn't look good."

I was getting hungry so I unzipped my cooler bag and pulled out my sandwich, but then Sherry held up a hand and said, "Stop right there, Eunice. Now, I know you prefer to eat at your desk — you're such a good worker — but we're having a Wendy meeting, and we all need to be there, no exceptions. You're coming with me to the cafeteria."

THE CAFETERIA SMELLED LIKE fish because it was Fish Fingers Day, Sherry told me when we walked in. How people can eat that greasy cafeteria food all the time I'll never be able to figure out, but I guess I got caught up in the excitement because the next thing I knew, I was lining up next to Sherry and pushing my orange tray along with hers, and there was tinsel and plastic holly everywhere because it was December, and the cafeteria ladies were jollying us along, and Sherry even offered to buy my lunch, but then she ended up not having enough money in her purse and actually needed me to lend her a couple of dollars, which I was more than happy to do, and I told her not to even think of paying me back.

And then Sherry led me over to her table ("This is where we always sit," she told me), and there was Val and Ruth P. and Ruth C. and Kevin and even Twyla, the temp, who'd only been in the office for two months, but there she was with all the rest of them.

"Everybody, look who the cat dragged in," said Sherry, as if she were making a joke.

"Ha ha," laughed Twyla, "I get it!"

"I thought you always ate lunch at your desk," Val said to me.

And Sherry said, "Eunice is my guest today."

That was too much for me, and I smiled, and Ruth C. said, "Look, Eunice is blushing!" And everybody at the table laughed, including me, and then Sherry got serious and said, "Okay gang, I brought Eunice up to speed so now we can all put our heads together. What I want us to do here is brainstorm as many ways as we can think of to cheer Wendy up." She put a hand over her mouth. "Oh, dear. Maybe *brainstorm* isn't the best word to use."

"Did you tell her about Wendy's apartment?" asked Ruth P. "The garbage bomb?"

Ruth P. is in charge of our Staff Fun bulletin board. She's a very social person.

"And the robe she was wearing, with the stains?" said Ruth C.

Ruth C. helps Ruth P. with the bulletin board. She supplies the tacks.

Sherry nodded in a solemn way. "I told her."

"Isn't it awful?" Twyla said to me in her high-pitched voice.

When Twyla first came to the office from her agency, Sherry said she had a face like a porpoise. She also has that high voice, and Sherry said she sounded like, "Scree, scree, scree!"

"Horrible," said Val.

Val's desk is next to mine, and she's the one who trained me on my reports. She and her husband do community theatre together, and she has two framed eight-by-tens of him next to her computer. He's a good-looking man, but those photos take up so much space, I can't figure out how she has any room to get her work done.

"It has to be cancer," said Kevin.

Kevin is very handsome. His hair is always neatly combed, and he only wears pants that have a bit of a sheen to them.

"Well, we'll see how she does," said Sherry. "We won't know for sure until they do the biopsy. In the meantime, she's staying in the hospital, and I think we should go and see her. We're all she has, remember — aside from our own little community, she doesn't have anybody. So I know she's hoping that her office family will come to visit."

"Oh my God." Val put her hands over her heart in a dramatic fashion. "She said that to you?"

"She didn't say that exactly. But I could see it in her eyes, as plain as day."

Twyla put down her fork and let out a high-pitched sob.

Sherry nodded. "We are all about Wendy now."

"I'll get a card from my desk," said Ruth P., who always does the cards for special occasions, "and we can all sign it."

"I'll get the pen," said Ruth C.

"We should bring flowers too," said Twyla, "and Get-Well-Soon balloons."

"And magazines," said Val.

"And a kitten!" said Kevin.

Everybody else looked at him like he was crazy, but I was nodding.

"What?" he said to them. "All sick people like kittens."

"He's got a point," I said.

"Are you crazy, Kevin?" said Ruth P., ignoring me. "How's she going to look after a kitten if she's in the hospital?"

"Ruth P. is right," said Sherry. "Wendy can't take care of herself, much less a baby animal."

"Fine." Kevin crossed his arms. "Then we can take turns looking after the kitten."

"I have an idea," said Sherry, and everyone looked at her. "I think we should all pitch in and take care of Wendy's apartment while she's in the hospital. We can bring in her mail and water her plants, and Lord knows the place could do with some tidying."

There was a brief silence, and then Twyla said, "Yesss," like air escaping from a tire.

Around the table, the others wagged their greasy plastic forks and congratulated Sherry on her idea.

I looked at the fish fingers on my plate and thought about how a year ago I would've taken them home to Johnny, when he used to have an appetite. "I'll help you with the kitten," I whispered to Kevin, and he smiled at me.

THE NEXT DAY, SHERRY and Val and Ruth P. went to visit Wendy on their lunch hour. I could've gone with them if I wanted to, but it was a Thursday and my reports are due on Friday, and the three of them were gone for more than an hour, and I can't afford that kind of time the day before I have to hand in my reports.

They brought Ruth P.'s card that we'd all signed with Ruth C.'s pen (I wrote, "Eat lots of Jell-O!" because I was trying to think of something nice associated with hospitals, and the fact that they often serve Jell-O was the only good thing that came to mind), and Sherry told me later that day that Wendy had been in good spirits. She was sitting up and joking with the gals about not having to do her weekly score sheets for Mr. Vanderhoeven. Wendy's score sheets are quantitative and my reports are qualitative — there's a big difference.

"Did you tell her about the kitten?" I said.

Sherry squinted. "No, I don't think we mentioned the kitten. But Wendy said our card was very thoughtful, and she really appreciated my idea about us keeping up her apartment while she wasn't there, but she said she'd like to wait for the biopsy results before we started that because she might be going home soon. She said she was hoping for the best." Sherry took a deep breath. "And then there were tears."

"Oh, no," I said. "Wendy started to cry?"

"No, I did. We've gotten so close, Wendy and me, and I

couldn't bear to see her lying in that hospital bed wearing that ratty nightgown of hers, surrounded by all sorts of equipment. Not that she's hooked up to any of it, but it's there, you know?"

I stood up then, and I put my arms around Sherry. *She feels so deeply about her friends,* I thought, *but who's feeling deeply about her?* So I hugged her and said, "Maybe there's still good news to come."

"Oh, Eunice," said Sherry, holding me, "I hope so."

A WEEK OR SO later, the biopsy came back positive for cancer, and do you know what Sherry did? She went right out to Sears and had copies of Wendy's keys cut for all of us, and then she went to the ladies' department and spent her own money on the nicest nightgown she could find and took it to Wendy along with some balloons, even though apparently Wendy said no, no, she was perfectly happy with the nightgown she already had and didn't need anything fancy.

But Sherry insisted on throwing out the old nightie because she said Wendy deserved something new and beautiful to brighten her dark days. And then Sherry sat with her all night and cried, even though Wendy told her she didn't mind being alone — she liked it, actually — because, Sherry said to me, who really likes being alone?

THE NEXT DAY, KEVIN went out and picked up a kitten from the Humane Society, and he and Twyla took him to the hospital to show Wendy.

I thought they would've asked me to go along, because everybody knows I have a lot of cat experience, and I know for a fact that Twyla doesn't even like animals because I once heard her telling a joke that went like this: "Taking a hamster to the vet is like taking a disposable lighter to get fixed." But they didn't ask me, so I couldn't help them.

Sherry told me Kevin said Wendy was sleeping at the time, but they snuggled that little ball of fur right up next to her and took a digital photo, which Kevin said he'd print out on his colour inkjet at home to show her when she was awake sometime. Then they took the kitten to Wendy's apartment — Sherry said she was pretty sure Wendy wasn't allergic — along with some food and a litter box.

Sherry told me all this in the early afternoon. The poor thing was exhausted from the night before, even though she'd slept in and come to work late, which isn't something I would've done but that's how Sherry is, she puts her friends first. Then she asked if I wanted to go along with her after work to bring in Wendy's mail and water her plants, and visit Andrew Lloyd Webber. Andrew Lloyd Webber is the name Kevin suggested for the kitten, because he noticed Wendy had a bunch of soundtracks to his musicals, including *Cats*.

"Of course," I said right away. "Of course I'll go with you, Sherry."

"Great, then it's all set." Sherry beamed at me, and I felt as if everything — my computer, my in-tray, my pen-and-pencil cage — was lit up by that smile on her face. "I'll come by your desk at five o'clock."

Ten minutes after she walked away, I remembered that I was supposed to take Johnny to the clinic that night.

Now, the thing about people is, they're unpredictable. You

think you know how they'll react to something, and then they go and prove you wrong, every time.

My Johnny, though, right from the start he was a different story. I'll admit he was a bit of a handful when I first brought him home. But then he was sweet as anything to me, twenty-four hours a day, or however many hours in a day we spent together. And I could count on him to be consistent.

But people — they'll turn around one day and act completely differently from how they acted before. There's simply no telling.

For example, when I went to Sherry's desk to explain that I couldn't go with her to Wendy's that night, I thought she'd understand. Especially since it had to do with Johnny and his not being well. But what she said was, "What do you mean you can't go?"

"I just can't," I said. "I'm sorry, Sherry. I guess in the heat of the moment I forgot about Johnny's appointment."

"Johnny, Johnny, Johnny," she said, in a not very nice tone of voice.

"What do you mean by that?"

"A cat can be replaced, Eunice. A person is forever."

Which is what people think, you know, who don't have pets. They think it doesn't matter. They think pets are disposable — you lose one, you buy another.

"Johnny is important to me," I said.

And she looked at me like I was a bug or I was stupid — like I was a stupid bug — and said, "Wendy is dying, Eunice. Our co-worker is dying, and there's nothing any of us can do about it, except maybe water her plants and bring in her mail and feed Andrew Lloyd Webber once in a while. Because she has nobody.

And you're standing there telling me you can't go because of Johnny."

The way she said his name again like that, it got to me. You know how things can get to you? So I looked at her and said, "Johnny is dying too, Sherry. And maybe that doesn't matter to you, but it matters to me."

Oh boy, you should've seen her face. She didn't know what to say to me after that!

And then I walked away.

THE NEXT DAY WAS a Friday so I had my reports to do, and I was also preoccupied with thinking about the night before.

The clinic had been decorated with garlands and plastic holly, and the vet had poked and prodded Johnny, and he didn't complain — he never was a complainer — but I could tell he was feeling anxious. Before we left, they recommended lots of rest, and I told them he'd been doing that already, and they said that's good, but then I caught the vet and the nurse exchanging a glance that they didn't think I saw.

I was also feeling bad for how short I'd been with Sherry the day before, because all she'd really wanted was my company, and all she wanted us to do was help a sick friend — a dying friend — together. I was planning on saying something nice to her when I went to deliver my reports, but she beat me to it.

She walked by on her way to lunch and stopped in front of my desk and smiled at me. "Eunice," she said in a very sincere voice, and I knew she was going to ask me about Johnny because Sherry is the type to look to the future and let bygones be bygones. "Eunice," she said, "how is your day going?"

"Oh, Sherry," I said and heard my voice catch, "he's not doing very well." Then I realized she hadn't asked about Johnny at all.

Sherry made a sad face where she stuck out her bottom lip and sort of folded it over her top lip, and she stared at me for a good fifteen seconds before I mustered up a smile and said, "Thanks for asking, Sherry."

"Well," she said with a wink, "you know me!"

I nodded and switched my gaze to the Grand Canyon. The way the edges of my computer screen framed that natural wonder, it humbled me to see it. *Johnny and I are specks*, I thought to myself. *We are teeny-tiny specks, the two of us.*

"So, about last night," said Sherry. "Eunice, oh my God, the state of that woman's apartment has to be seen to be believed. When I went to take her to the hospital that first time, I wasn't paying much attention because I was all about Wendy, but last night when Twyla and I went over —"

"Wait a minute, you went with Twyla?" I said. "But she's a temp. And you always said she had a porpoise face."

Sherry nodded, shrugged. "You missed your chance."

I didn't know what to say to that, so I took the top piece of bread off my ham sandwich and contemplated the round pink slice inside. The ham was slightly shiny, with that hint of a rainbow that lunchmeat can sometimes get.

"Anyway, there wasn't any mail and Wendy doesn't have any plants, so we just put some food in Andrew Lloyd Webber's bowl and —"

I looked up at her. "Wet or dry?"

"What?"

"The cat food. Was it wet or dry?"

She sighed an impatient sigh. "I don't know, Twyla fed him. But I'm telling you, Eunice, I don't think Wendy ever used a mop or a broom once in that place. I guess there was all that time she wasn't feeling well, but it takes years for a home to get like that."

Sherry doesn't have any pets and couldn't be expected to know about these things, so I explained it to her. "Because you should really be giving him dry food most of the time, so he gets used to it."

"Twyla and I looked around for some cleaning supplies, but we couldn't find any in her closets, and we didn't want to go snooping around, so we just tidied up as best we could."

I'd been adding flaxseed oil to Johnny's dry food (which I mashed for him until it was soft) because I'd read on a holistic pet-health website that it was good for the cells, but I don't think it ever did anything for him. "You should only give him the wet food as a treat," I said. "The wet food isn't as healthy as the dry food. They're easy to tell apart — the wet food is wet, and the dry food looks like little hearts, but brown."

Sherry waved a hand. "That's all well and good, Eunice, but I can't concern myself with cat food at a time like this, with a woman's life — our co-worker's life — hanging in the balance." Then she stopped talking and looked at me, waiting for me to say something.

So I said, "Sherry, you are a good person. You're so good, to me and Wendy and everybody. And I'm not even — I'm different from you, but I wish I wasn't. I wish I was the same as you, but I'm not."

"Well, thank God for that!" she said, and smiled. "Thank God we're different, Eunice, because that's what makes us such a great team!" Then she clapped her hands together. "Now, bring that sandwich. You're coming to the cafeteria with me!"

"I wish I could, Sherry," I said, "but it's Friday, and I have to finish my reports."

"Come on then, chop chop!" she said, as if she hadn't heard what I'd told her.

"I can't, Sherry."

And she gave me this sudden, sad look, and said, "Oh, all right, then." Before heading off, she glanced around and seemed confused for a second, as if she'd forgotten where she was going.

AFTER THAT, THE WEEKS went by and the days got colder and Christmas came and went, and the whole time Johnny and Wendy got sicker.

Ruth P. had the idea to prop up a big framed photo of Wendy on Wendy's empty desk. She made sure there was a fresh card next to it every Monday for people to write their up-to-the-minute get-well wishes, and at the end of each week, the cards were delivered to Wendy's hospital room.

The only pre-cancer photo of Wendy they could find was from an old staff potluck, which had been up on the Staff Fun bulletin board. It was a crowd shot, and Ruth P. had had it enlarged, so it was kind of grainy. It showed Wendy holding a plate of food, her mouth open to receive a cocktail shrimp, tail-first.

"That's Wendy," I overheard someone say when I passed by with my reports one day. "She was always doing things backwards." They were starting to talk about her as if she were already dead.

I had a standing invitation to the cafeteria from Sherry by this time, but I only took her up on it for a few lunches early on. Then I started going home at noon to feed Johnny, because he was at the point where all he would take was liquid vitamins out of an eyedropper.

I don't think Sherry missed me anyway. She'd become pretty busy with her charity fundraising (she convinced Mr. Vanderhoeven to shave his head for cancer!) and her new job responsibilities (she'd volunteered to do Wendy's score sheets for her same pay, but she said Mr. Vanderhoeven said that kind of initiative deserved a raise).

Then one Friday, the whole big group of them — Sherry, Val, Ruth P., Ruth C., Kevin, and Twyla — came by my desk on their way to the cafeteria.

I was closing down my computer because I wasn't coming back after lunch. That morning Johnny had been quieter than usual, and I had a bad feeling, so I finished my reports early and asked Mr. Vanderhoeven if I could have the afternoon off, and he said yes. So I was ready to leave, but then the six of them were hovering over my desk, looking down at me.

"Hi, Eunice," said Sherry.

"Hi, Sherry," I said. "Hi, everybody."

"We haven't seen you in the cafeteria in a while," said Val.

"Oh, you know." I shrugged. "I've been going home to Johnny lately."

"Did you sign Wendy's card this week?" asked Ruth P.

"Hmm, I don't think I have," I said.

"Well," said Ruth C., "it's there. I put a new pen out today."

"How's she doing?" I asked them.

Kevin sighed. "I printed out the photo of her and Andrew Lloyd Webber, and I brought it to her last week, but she was sleeping again so I taped it up on the wall by her bed. She didn't look good."

"I saw her this morning," said Sherry, "and I brought her some crossword puzzles, because I know she loves her crossword puzzles, and she looked positively gaunt." She frowned at me. "When's the last time you saw her, Eunice?"

I looked up at all of them there waiting for my answer, and I didn't say anything.

"Have you even been to visit her once?"

"I have to get going." I stood up. "I have to get home to Johnny. I finished my reports already, and Mr. Vanderhoeven knows I'm going home."

"We don't care about your reports," said Sherry. "We care about Wendy. We are all about people around here, Eunice, in case you didn't notice."

"That's fine for you," I said to her, "but I've got Johnny."

And Sherry looked at me, and I couldn't believe it, but there wasn't a trace of sympathy in her eyes. "Eunice," she said, "he's just a cat."

And I thought I was going to start crying right there in front of everybody, but the tears didn't come. I just faced them all across my desk, and I didn't say a word.

Sherry's nostrils flared — I could see them, she was that close. "I don't think you should come to the cafeteria with us today, Eunice."

I didn't say anything to that, either.

"Let's go, gang," she said, and they went off down the hall together in a tight little clump.

JOHNNY WAS DEAD WHEN I got home.

I opened the door, and do you know what? I knew. I couldn't feel him anymore, is the only way I can describe it. You might think that's crazy, but that's the way it was.

After a while, I found him in the coat closet, curled up in the back corner. He hardly took up any room — he was the smallest I'd seen him since he was a kitten. I crawled in there with him and took one of his tiny paws between my fingers, and I thought of little Andrew Lloyd Webber all alone in Wendy's empty apartment. And I started to cry. I cried for him, and I cried for all the cats in the world who don't have love, and at least that's one thing Johnny had. You can take everything else away, but at the very least he had love.

THAT NIGHT MY PHONE rang, and it was Sherry, which is funny because I couldn't remember ever giving her my home number.

"I've been calling everyone." She sounded out of breath. "Something awful's happened."

"Oh, no," I said. "Is it Wendy?"

"Oh, Eunice," she said, and that's when I heard the catch in her voice, and a second later, she was sobbing.

"Shhh," I said. "It's okay. Let it out."

By this time, I'd taken Johnny to the vet. I'd said goodbye to him, and the nurse had given me a big hug, and then I'd come home to my empty apartment.

"Wendy, she —"

"I know. I know it's hard. Shhh."

"She said she doesn't want me to visit her anymore!" Sherry wailed.

"What?"

"After everything I've done for her. How could she, Eunice?"

And Lord forgive me, but do you know what I did? I laughed. Loud. It came out of my mouth, and there was no holding it back.

"Are you," said Sherry, "are you laughing at me?"

"No," I said, giggling.

"This isn't a joke, Eunice!"

"I know!" I chuckled.

And she hung up. The line went dead, and Wendy was still alive, and Sherry was probably really upset with me, and I just couldn't stop laughing.

THE NEXT DAY, I took my set of keys and went over to Wendy's apartment. I was expecting the place to be a disaster like everybody said, but it really wasn't that bad. Maybe it wasn't up to Sherry's standards because she lives in a condo with a balcony and a communal party room, but it looked nice enough to me. It was too quiet, though, so I looked through Wendy's CD collection for something to put on, and the soundtrack to *Cats* jumped right out at me.

After a while, I found Andrew Lloyd Webber under a couch and coaxed him out by opening a can of wet food in the kitchen. He came running, and I scooped him up in my arms, and I pushed my face into his fur, which was even softer than Johnny's had been, if you can believe that.

Then I was crying, and Andrew Lloyd Webber was meow-ing — cry, meow, cry, meow — and we kept going like that for a while, with "Mr. Mistoffelees" playing in the background and lifting both of our hearts.

And the whole time he didn't try to jump down once. He stayed in my arms and let me hold him, even with that can of wet food on the floor smelling so darn good.

HALFWAY TO THE HOSPITAL, I realized I didn't have anything to bring Wendy, so I stopped in at a drug store and picked up a card. The card didn't have any words in it, just a cartoon of a sun peeking out over the top of a cloud. Because what is there to say?

I asked for Wendy's room number at the front desk, and I took the elevator up, and I walked down the hall until I found her door, which was open. And there she was.

Wendy was propped up on pillows, and her eyes were closed. She seemed so small and frail in her fancy, frilly nightgown, and her skin was yellow and her hair was matted and the streaks had grown out so the ends were a totally different colour from her roots. Every corner of the room was filled with gifts that were completely useless to her — wilted flowers and shrivelled Get-Well-Soon balloons and unopened magazines and untouched crossword puzzles, and above everything else was the photo of Andrew Lloyd Webber staring down at her like a guardian angel.

I stood there in the doorway looking at her, and for the life of me, I couldn't think of anything to say except, "Hi, Wendy."

For a long while, she didn't answer me, and I thought maybe she was napping and maybe I should leave. But I had Andrew Lloyd Webber pressed against me under my coat, and I thought

I should get her permission to take him home, even though at the same time I was thinking, *What's she going to do with him? She can't take care of herself, much less a baby animal.*

Then she opened her eyes.

"It's me, Eunice," I said quickly, "from work. I sit next to Val?"

"I know who you are," she said in a quiet but steady voice. "Come in."

"I brought this for you." I walked into the room and handed her the card.

"Thanks," she whispered. "Could you put it over there?"

"Okay." I held it up for her. "It doesn't have any words in it. It's just got a picture of a sun, and there's a cloud, and the sun's peeking over it." I set it down in the field of cards on her bedside table.

"They keep bringing me all these things." Wendy gestured around her with a slim, yellow hand. "I'm running out of room here, but they keep on bringing stuff. That cat photo showed up last week. Somebody came in and took my picture with a cat when I was sleeping."

"That's nice," I said.

"Nice? It's weird. And I don't even like cats."

I took a few steps closer. "You don't?"

She shook her head. "I'm allergic."

I felt Andrew Lloyd Webber's soft warmth on my chest, and my heart was soaring now, but I forced myself to look nonchalant and said, "Oh."

Then Wendy's face went serious, and she reached up and touched my arm. Her hand was light as a feather. "Sorry, I forgot you have a cat. How's it doing? Sherry told me it wasn't well."

"No, he's —" And then I stopped.

"Go ahead." She made a gun out of her thumb and forefinger and pointed it at me — Sherry always said she had a goofy sense of humour — and said, "Shoot."

"Oh, Wendy." I took a deep breath. "Johnny died."

And she gave me the saddest and kindest look I've ever seen, and put her hand back on my arm. "I am really sorry to hear that, Eunice."

"Thank you." I blinked at her. "Sherry told you he was sick?"

"Yeah, but she didn't exactly say it in a nice way." Wendy scowled and tugged at the lacy ruffles around her neck. "Jesus God, I hate this nightie."

And right then I remembered I had something else for her. I reached into my purse and took out her apartment keys and placed them on her cluttered bedside table. "These are yours."

"Thanks, Eunice. I appreciate that." She smiled at me and closed her eyes.

I smiled too, and I wanted so desperately to take back every not-nice thought I'd ever had about Wendy. Because she was a real person. She was the realest person I'd ever met. And past the sharp angle of her shoulder, I could see that cartoon sun peeking over that cartoon cloud, and I thought to myself, *Spring is coming.*

Right at that moment, Andrew Lloyd Webber meowed.

Then he poked his small, fluffy head out the top of my coat, and Wendy's eyes flew open, and she sneezed and her whole body quaked from it. She looked at Andrew Lloyd Webber and looked at the photo of her and him on the wall. Then she sneezed again and said, "What the hell?"

I quickly handed her the Kleenex box from her bedside table, knocking over some of the cards, including mine.

"Meow," Andrew Lloyd Webber said again in his sweet, angelic kitten-voice.

Wendy grabbed a tissue and waved it at us like a flag. "Get that thing out of here, will you?" she told me before blowing her nose.

"I will," I said. "Thank you, Wendy." And we backed out of the room and left her alone, which was all she ever wanted, anyway.

And Also Sharks

Oh my God Janet, you are so brave. Your bravery astounds me. Because you lay yourself bare for the world when you put your feelings out there to be known. But just basically because your words touch so many people, and there are so many of us who are suffering from the self-esteem issues that affect our very lives. So I guess what I'm saying here is that you are doing something extremely BRAVE.

Plus that recipe you shared on your last post for the ham casserole with white sauce is AMAZING! I made it the other day and it was so easy, exactly like you said it would be, and I was supposed to have my brother and his wife over for dinner and that was what I was going to serve, and they were going to bring a salad which I think was going to be a macaroni salad. But then they called at the last minute and said they couldn't make it because her pregnancy was acting up, which I guess you have to understand, pregnancies being the way they are.

But anyway, the casserole. You said it would nourish the soul, the making part and the eating part, and like you always are, you were right. Last week I did the exercise you suggested where you cut out pictures from magazines that appeal to you, and paste them onto a piece of paper to make a collage which represents how you want your life to be, but all I had at home were a bunch of Reader's Digests and an old copy of National Geographic which was the Shark Issue, so my collage ended up being about this family that got trapped by an avalanche and also sharks.

So after I got that very disappointing call from my brother, I reframed the situation like you say to do, like how you can make an ugly painting look beautiful with a beautiful frame, and I thought about how extremely lucky I was that I was going to have so many leftovers. Even though I was really looking forward to that macaroni salad.

I lit some candles in my strength corners and I sat down at the table with the casserole, and I inhaled deeply and closed my eyes to savour the first bite, and do you know what was weird? It was so weird but the first thing that came to my mind was my mother. She looked like an angel. So I thought, There's my mother, I guess I should give her a call. So I called her up and said to her, "Hey, I've got this ham casserole with white sauce and it serves four, do you want some? I'm all alone over here with this ham casserole." And she said, "I'd love to honey, really, but I've got this comedy show buffet. It's a comedy show with a buffet? And then your stepdad and I are going to the Polish Combatants Hall." So I said, "Fine, Mom, do what you want, you always do." And she said, "What is that supposed to mean?" And I said, "Nothing. I have to go, my casserole is getting cold."

Anyway, Janet, what I really want to tell you is that I really respect your opinion and what you have to say, but most of all your bravery. You are not afraid to state your opinions, even when some people put comments like Kate P. did last week, though in a very small way I have to say I agree a little bit with what she put about your post that talked about adding a dash of joy to your daily routine, which is not so easy for everyone although you made it sound easy.

But my main message here is that I wanted you to know that there are those of us who read Planet Janet that believe what you say is TRUE and BRAVE. You keep putting yourself and your opinions — and your recipes for white-sauce casseroles and two-step stews and sinfully gooey desserts! — out there. And Janet if we all had your guts then I am proud to say that this world would be a better place. But we don't and basically the world is a harsh reality for those people who choose to live in it.

The photo of the avalanche family, it was taken after the fact. So it was all staged because of course a professional photographer wasn't with them when the avalanche happened. They're all hugging each other and at the same time sort of hugging themselves, to give the impression they need to for warmth, is I guess the idea. And then there's the photo of an avalanche actually happening, but it wouldn't have been THEIR avalanche, just an avalanche wherever. With the purpose being to show all that snow cascading down, which apparently that's all an avalanche is — just unstable layers of snow letting go.

I would hate to be trapped in an avalanche, wouldn't you? God, that would be awful. All that pressure, all that snow pushing down on you. Apparently the sheer weight of dense snow makes it very difficult to breathe, and it takes only three minutes for a person to die from suffocation. I did some Internet research on this stuff, that's how I know, in case you were wondering. And this family SURVIVED! The daughter lost a toe to frostbite, but that's pretty much it for lasting damage. And I'm sure all of them will have terrifying nightmares forever. But everybody gets nightmares, don't they?

The way the family survived was they created air pockets for themselves. There was so little air for four people, and yet nobody hogged it. They shared their body warmth too — they huddled very close together, protecting each other. And do you know what this family said in the interview? "We remained calm, and we waited." How could they do that? Who ARE these people? But who knows if they were telling the truth, since nobody wants to look like a jerk in a Reader's Digest interview.

My mother's voice does this thing where you can always tell when she's lying. Kind of a gulping noise that you can detect at the end of her sentences. And I heard it when I called her about the ham casserole, so I don't know, maybe she wasn't actually going to the comedy show buffet and then the Polish Combatants Hall with my stepdad, who is not the most reliable person either, but that's another story.

Then there's the shark, which is a Great White, and he's got his mouth wide open so you see these rows and rows of deadly sharp teeth. And so smooth, like the white sauce — it had lumps in it at first, but I used a fork to stir it, like you said to, and eventually the lumps went away, and I found that whole process very rewarding. I guess that's why they call it comfort food.

So there was this husband, and he heard his wife screaming and that's when he saw the fin and he ran down the beach, and he dove into the ocean and he was yelling at her to "Swim! Swim away!" And she did and do you know that it was actually HIM that got bitten? The shark was after her but the husband put himself between this truly fearsome predator and his wife, and the shark grabbed him by the torso — that's how large this shark's jaws were, they could go around a man's TORSO! — and isn't that amazing, I mean that a person would save another person from a shark, I mean a SHARK! Isn't that one of the number-one fears in the world? It must be way up there anyway, and this man put himself in that shark's path to save his wife. And now he has this long scar from it, which his wife probably kisses all the time, gets down on her knees and kisses that scar all over, at least I hope she does — I would if I was her, I would be so grateful. It's something else, Janet, I'm telling you. This man was in a shark's MOUTH and he SURVIVED! It's an awe-striking fact when you take the time to think about it.

I guess what I'm trying to get at here is that nobody else says the things you say, Janet. You have a way with words, that's for sure. Myself, it takes me a lot longer to get my point across. But what do I have to say? I've never been trapped in an avalanche or bitten by a shark or anything like that. I live a pretty ordinary life. Though I wonder how brave YOU would be in the face of a Great White Shark. I like to think you would save all of us, that you would throw yourself in the path of the Great White Shark that is all of our self-esteem problems. But somehow I doubt it. You are wrestling with your own demons and I can accept that.

But it is so HARD, Janet, and you know what it's like, I can tell. I know that you know how we all feel. I try my utmost to stay on track, every day. I get up and I have my routine and at the end of the day I go to bed. And I understand, like you tell us, that it's all a process. But sometimes I just lie there and imagine what it would be like to be trapped by an avalanche or bitten in half by a Great White Shark. But then I think, I can avoid both of those things. Easily. A) Don't go on mountains. B) Don't go in oceans.

I do try to be good to my self, Janet. I try to take comfort from the everyday and eat comfort foods and say comforting things to myself, reassuring and self-affirming things. And yet it's very hard to stay positive, as you well know. Or do you, Janet? You can read all of our comments here and know that you're not alone in this cold world. You are not alone on Planet Janet, because we are all there with you.

Apparently with some shark attacks, you can hear your own bones snap in the shark's mouth. Now that is SOMETHING. And the thing is, a shark may bite a human out of hunger, but just as often, it'll bite out of simple curiosity. Just to see what we taste like.

And the thing about my brother is, is that I have doubts, and I mean serious doubts, that he would ever save his wife, pregnant or not, from a shark. He loves her, sure, we all love her. She's very personable. Which is why I was additionally surprised and saddened when they called and cancelled on our dinner plans at the last minute. But I guess with babies involved there's no telling. And my brother adores this woman, there's no getting around that. Still, if he saw a fin in the same water she was in, would he dive in and swim towards it, or would he run the other way? You tell me.

Maybe on Planet Janet there are no sharks, and maybe there are no avalanches, but some day there might be. Some day it will snow on your mountains and your oceans will fill up with fins. Something that shark-attack victims often say is: "It came out of nowhere." Actually, that's what avalanche victims say too. It makes you think, doesn't it?

But really overall there are so many of us who support you, Janet, and your daily struggles with self-esteem. And I am here to say, for once and for all, that your life will get better. It will get better, Janet, I promise you. It has to.

Coconut

SHELLEY STARTS SHOPLIFTING AS soon as she gets back from the all-inclusive resort because she already misses the way she could just take whatever she wanted.

On her way home from Pearson, she asks the airport limo driver to drop her off at Zellers. She wheels her suitcase up and down the aisles, and a man with a big *Z* on his chest smiles and asks her, "Are you coming or going?"

She is eyeing the large bag of coconut macaroons behind his head. She smiles back and tells him that she has just returned from a week in Cuba.

"Oh yeah? I went to Cuba once. Where did you stay?"

She tells him Breezes Varadaro.

"Package deal. Sweet." Then he says, "Would you like to have a drink some time, with me?"

She says, "Only if it's all-inclusive." They both laugh. She gives him a fake number and he steps aside so she can reach the bag of macaroons.

When she is in the next aisle over, she puts it in her suitcase.

LATER ON, SHELLEY IS in her living room listening to the CD she bought for ten pesos from one of the bands that played during dinner at Jimmy's Buffet. She taps her tanned foot to the beat and eats macaroons.

She mixes herself a Cuba Libre, which is basically a rum and Coke but tastes better when it's called a *Cuba Libre*. She sees a spider running up the wall and squashes it with her bare hand, which is something she has never done before. At the resort, she saw a dead tarantula on the floor outside her room — someone had stepped on it.

At the resort, she drank all day and danced all night and swam in the ocean, where she worried about sharks at first but as the week went on she worried less, and by the end she had no worries at all.

BEFORE SHELLEY WENT TO Cuba, she went for shawarma with her then-boyfriend TJ. They ordered two combos and he took the tray to a table while she paid for their food. Next to the cash register was a sign that read, "You could win a free bag of gourmet potato chips!"

"Hey," Shelley said to the girl behind the counter, "do I have to fill out a ballot or something for those chips?"

The girl glanced at the sign. "Oh," she said, "that's over." She took Shelley's money and tossed the sign into the recycling bin.

When Shelley sat down with TJ, he picked up a newspaper from the empty table beside theirs and started reading it.

She ate quietly for a few minutes, then pulled her can of Lebanese pop closer and stared at the Lebanese words on the label. The foreign letters were loving arms, curved and outstretched.

TJ said to her, "This isn't working out."

And she knew he felt this way because of a conversation he'd had with his best friend Wade a few days before, which she had overheard.

TJ and Wade were grilling steakettes on TJ's patio. Shelley was adding the pea layer to her layered pasta salad on the other side of the sliding glass doors, which weren't closed all the way, although TJ and Wade seemed to think they were, and Wade said to TJ, "Shelley's boobs aren't as big as you think they are."

TJ said, "What the hell are you talking about?"

"Padded bra, dude."

Shelley looked down at her chest, which was flecked with light Italian dressing.

"You can tell when it's cold out." Wade made a fist and popped one finger out, then tucked it back in. "How long's it been now with you two — a week?"

"Three weeks," said TJ.

"You should really know this stuff by now." Wade shook his head and flipped a steakette, and the flat patty sizzled when it landed.

Shelley hadn't been worried at the time because she had met TJ at a party where Wade went to the bathroom and all the guests put their fingers to their lips and winked big winks at each other and then headed down to basement.

Everybody huddled together and went quiet and they could all hear Wade's footsteps overhead, crossing from one end of the room to the other. "Guys?" he called.

SHELLEY UNPACKS AND DOES laundry, and then she takes her empty suitcase to The Bay.

In the shows the resort put on at night for a sunburned audience in rows of sticky plastic chairs, local women danced on stage in costumes that were only three small white circles and one thin white string.

In the ocean, two glistening twenty-year-old boys threw a Frisbee back and forth over the heads of other swimmers. The dark-haired one yelled at the blond one to "Dive, mother-fucker! What is wrong with you?" And the blond one yelled back, "Fuck, no! Every time I dive I get a mouthful of this fucking salt water."

In the cosmetics section, Shelley slips a bottle of Soothing Coconut Emollient into her suitcase.

SHE IS ALSO IN major debt from the trip. She tried saving up for it, but in the end she just put it on her credit card. One thing she did to economize before she left was buy a cheaper brand of face cream.

"The thing is," the Shoppers cosmetics girl said to her when she brought the product to the register, "if you switch moistur-izers, you're going to get into trouble. Because your skin is an organ. Like, you can change your hair product and it's no problem. But with your skin, because it is an organ, if you use a new product — especially one with lots of fillers, like that one — your skin can and will go into shock. And you do not want that."

"But it says it's for sensitive skin," said Shelley.

The girl looked at her, unblinking. "Do you really believe that?"

On the subway ride home, Shelley read the back of her new face-cream bottle. *Discontinue use if signs of irritation occur. If irritation persists, consult your doctor.*

In her bathroom, she applied the lotion and waited in front of the mirror to see if anything out of the ordinary would happen, but nothing did.

OVER THE WEEK, SHELLEY shoplifts some moisturizing coconut sunscreen, a coconut-scented air freshener, and a padded bra (which she needs, but does not actually *need*-need).

Then one day she's on the sidewalk following a mother and her very small child. The boy is probably less than a year old — not an infant anymore but not a toddler yet either. Mostly a baby, still. He is slow and unsteady on his feet, and the mother says to him, "I love you but I haven't got all day here." She lets go of his hand to look in a store window.

Shelley has always thought, "How easy," when she's seen little kids waddling ahead of their distracted parents, and it is. It's super easy. She just picks him up and walks left, and when she is halfway down the street she hears the mother screaming, and then she is in her apartment with somebody else's child, who doesn't seem to mind very much.

The baby walks on his wobbly legs around her living room and makes soft "ooga" sounds. Shelley sits down on her couch and watches him explore. She could get used to this.

THE THING ABOUT SHELLEY is, she really likes shopping a lot.

One time she spotted a sign outside a church advertising a designer sample sale, and before she realized the sale wasn't until the next day, she ran up the stairs and pushed open the big church door and looked inside. Then she sighed and slumped and turned away because there was nothing there except empty pews, stained-glass windows, Jesus on a cross, and disappointment.

On their first date, TJ took her to a scenic lookout with a view of the city all laid out in a panoramic way, and he put his arms around her and they gazed out over all the scenes, and neither of them said anything for a while and then Shelley said, "I wonder if they have a gift shop."

He said, "But Shelley, it's nature."

She said, "Yeah, but maybe I can get like a belt buckle or something."

THE LITTLE BOY IS curious about everything, and really seems to listen when Shelley says things to him. She wants to tell him a story but she doesn't have any kids' books.

TJ told her a story once about when he and Wade and some other guys kidnapped a penguin from the zoo and took it back to their apartment and kept it in the bathtub. They fed it tuna and gave it showers so it stayed wet, but eventually it died. When it started to smell, they dumped it off in front of the zoo gates in the middle of the night and drove off.

But she figures that isn't a good story to tell a baby.

Then she remembers that the best thing TJ ever did for her was on the subway when someone let a serious one rip, he pulled a pack of spearmint gum out of his bag and held it under her nose. "Smell this," he said. "Breathe in deep."

She tells this to the baby and he seems to understand. His big blue eyes are full of wisdom. She could look at those eyes for days.

"Do you know what I want right now?" she asks him.

"Ooga," he says.

"Anything fake maple. Like a maple candy or cookie or whatever. It can't be real maple, though. It has to be fake."

"Ooga."

"I am picking up what you are putting down, Baby."

SHELLEY TAKES THE BABY and her suitcase to the store for tourists in the mall.

"God, this place is stupid," she tells him.

He drools at her, and she squeezes his hand. His whole hand fits inside the palm of her hand, it's so small.

Shelley lets him wander around while she stands in front of a shelf of miniature jugs advertising "Real Canadian Maple Syrup." She shakes her head. "This is not what I want."

"Is that your baby?" the store clerk says from behind her counter. "You can't just let a baby walk around in here."

"He's not —" Shelley starts to say, and then there is a crash.

The boy has knocked over a display of ceramic polar bears that are dressed up like Mounties.

The store clerk starts to head their way but Shelley tucks the little guy up under her arm and they get out fast.

"Eat our dust, Canadiana," she whispers into his tiny pink seashell ear.

"I'M GOING TO CALL you Davis," Shelley tells the baby in the food court.

He squeezes the fries he is holding into a paste and then mashes the paste into his mouth.

"I think this is healthy, Davis — I think I'm transitioning. Because before all I wanted was coconut, and now I'm craving maple. You see what I'm saying to you?"

"Ooga."

She reaches out to steady him before he falls off his chair. "Whoa, Davis, that was a close one! You are a lucky duck."

Then she hears, "Shelley!" She looks over and it's her friend Monique, who is a hugger and a fake-smiler.

Monique hugs and fake-smiles at Shelley and then she crosses her arms and makes a pouty face at Davis. "And who is this?"

"That's Davis," says Shelley. "I'm babysitting."

"Aren't you a little old to be a sitter?" says Monique. "Don't you think you're maybe at the age where you should be look-ing after your own baby?" She jerks the handle of the giant stroller she is pushing, and says to the tiny girl inside, "Wake up, Dee-Dee."

Monique got married a few years ago and she used to say things to her husband Corey like, "Corey, I love that neither of us got super drunk at our wedding." And Corey would go, "Yeah, Monique. I love you." Then they had a kid and got divorced right after.

Now Monique gets a babysitter so she and Shelley can go tanning and then go out to the bars. One time there was this guy Monique had made out with before and gave her number to, and she got a text from him saying, "Where U at?" So she texted him the bar name and he said he was on his way over, and Monique giggled to Shelley, "Okay, where do you think he lives, honestly? To come all this way?" Shelley said, "You don't know where he lives?" And Monique said, "I just went to the bathroom and someone wrote on the door, 'Don't drink from the mainstream,' and I thought, 'Yeah, that's me.'"

Monique frowns at Shelley. "What's with the suitcase?"

Shelley shrugs. "It's like my shopping cart."

"Hey, that reminds me, I got to get my CD back from you. Dee-Dee misses the maracas." Monique pushes the stroller over to Davis's chair, and her little girl looks up at the little boy.

Shelley pokes Davis. "Say hello to Dee-Dee, Davis."

"Ooga," says Davis.

Dee-Dee coos.

"Look at that," says Shelley. "They like each other."

SHELLEY AND DAVIS TAKE the bus home, and Shelley remembers the air-conditioned tour bus that took her to Havana. The tour guide's P.A. system was broken and Shelley was sitting in the back where the road sounds were the loudest, so only random words and phrases came through: "Pirates." "Shops and restaurants." "Che Guevara." "Very nice drink."

On Shelley and Davis's bus, two tourists are filming each other and their surroundings. "This is downtown Toronto!" one of them says to the camera. "There is the Toronto Eaton Centre! And here is a cute Toronto baby!" They turn the camera on Davis, who spits up some partially digested fries.

Shelley shakes her head. "You're too young for embarrassment, aren't you, Davis?"

People did a lot of videotaping in Cuba — girls wearing bikinis, kids building sandcastles, geckos scurrying across floors. At the resort one night at dinner, a husband with a camcorder tracked his wife's movements through the buffet.

He followed her from the vegetable table, where she used tongs to pluck five individual cucumber slices out of a bowl and onto her plate, to the meat area, where she requested a "not pink" slice of roast beef, and finally to the pasta station, where she asked for "bow ties in the red sauce."

The cook opened a yellow package and dumped the contents into boiling water, and they all waited for a few minutes while the steam billowed, and then the cook fished out a single wobbly bow tie and tested it by putting it between his teeth and biting down softly, and the wife said, "Oh. Oh. Is that how you do it here?"

The husband said, "Alison, whoa." He laughed but his camera wobbled.

Then the cook ladled out the red sauce and made a cross over the pale noodles — first one line, then another. He handed the plate to the woman with a wink, and she took it and giggled and headed back to the tables where the band was playing *Oye Como Va* again.

The husband stood there filming the cook until the cook said, "You want something?" The husband said, "No, thank you." He turned off the camera, picked up an empty plate, and walked away.

Davis makes a sound in his diaper. It smells.

"Oh, God!" says Shelley. "Was that you?"

"LET'S PRETEND WE'RE MILLIONAIRES," Shelley tells Davis in the baby products aisle of Shoppers. "If you could have any brand of diapers in the world, what brand would that be?"

Davis reaches over and slaps his small hand against a package of Huggies.

Shelley pulls the diapers off the shelf and zips them into her suitcase. "I will make all of your wishes come true."

WHEN THEY GET HOME, Shelley puts Davis in the bathtub and turns on the water.

She says, "I'm trying to remember how old I was when I first learned to float."

"Ooga."

"Yeah, I can't remember. Older than you, probably."

She fills the tub about halfway, and then she squeezes a wet washcloth over Davis's head and he gurgles, and she shows him how to splash and he loves it. She tells him that a shampoo bottle is a boat and he actually seems to believe her.

"Soon enough, Davis, you will no longer believe," she says, and floats the shampoo bottle around him and makes "toot-toot" noises.

"Are you clean yet?" She sniffs him and makes a face. "I don't think regular soap is doing the job here — we'll have to bring in the big guns. Hold on, I'll be right back."

She leaves the bathroom, and when she comes back with a shoplifted bottle of coconut-scented dish soap that promises "Deep Cleaning Power and a Getaway from the Everyday," Davis is face-down in the tub.

One morning, the gardeners set up a table by the pool and

hacked open coconuts with a machete and poured rum inside for the tourists. Shelley drank hers on the spot and then asked them, "Would they cut —" and made a chopping motion with her hand on her coconut and put an extra peso on the tip plate. The head gardener winked at her and took her coconut and raised his machete and brought it down. He put the split halves in her hands and pried out the white meat with a butter knife. He knew what he was doing.

"Oh my God," Shelley says, and lifts the rubbery baby out of the water and gives him a little shake.

He coughs and sputters and fights for breath, and when he starts inhaling and exhaling properly she tells him, "Do not do that again, okay?"

"Ooga," Davis wheezes.

AFTER THEY'D BEEN DATING for maybe a week, TJ took Shelley to a restaurant where people ate in the dark.

The hostess hooked their elbows with hers and escorted them to their table. She sat them across from each other and left them alone in the pitch-blackness.

TJ reached over and took Shelley's hand, and Shelley screamed. She said, "I thought you were a spider."

"Isn't this place fancy?" he asked her.

"How can you tell?"

A waiter came over and said, "Would you like something to drink?"

Shelley jumped at his voice. "How do you find your way around in here?"

"I'm blind."

"Cool," said TJ.

They ordered wine, and the waiter's footsteps faded out, like in a radio play.

"I read a review of this place in the *Globe*," said TJ. "It's supposed to be amazing."

"But we won't be able to read the menu. We won't be able to see our food."

The other diners' conversations filled the air around them, and smells from other people's plates filled Shelley's nose. She gripped the edge of the table and felt a wad of gum or something else stuck underneath. Across from her, TJ was there but he wasn't. "I don't like this," she said.

TJ pushed his chair back and came around to her side. "Take my arm," he told her. "I have awesome night vision."

SHELLEY SHOPLIFTS A COCONUT cake mix from the grocery store. Back at home, she bakes the cake and lets it cool on the counter. She puts it on a plate, spreads the icing on thick, and sprinkles shredded coconut on top. Then she places the whole thing on the floor, in front of Davis.

He stares at the cake for a minute or so, gums chomping. Then he leans forward and sticks his entire face smack into the middle of it.

There was a newlywed couple at the resort who held hands all the time, even when it was inconvenient. Shelley saw them one day at the foot-washing station, and their clasped hands turned their foot washing into a game of Twister.

On her last night at the resort, Shelley danced with a succession of drunken college boys at the disco and let each one feel her up more aggressively than the last. By the end of the night, she had taken off her bra and hung it around her neck like a goose she had killed.

The next morning, she sat behind the newlywed couple on the bus to the airport and their heads bobbed together like the sparrows over the Cuban sandwich crumbs at lunch.

"I was really having this craving to go out and get a cake mix and then bake the cake and share it with somebody special," Shelley says to Davis, who is covered in icing. "You have made that dream a reality."

THE THING WAS, EVERYTHING was good but then everything was not good. TJ was starting to act different even before they had the shawarma.

It was to the point where Shelley had a feeling something was wrong, and by the end of their three weeks when she made up TJ's peanut butter sandwiches for him to take to work, she wasn't bothering to spread the peanut butter in an even layer. The way she did it was, there were places with no peanut butter at all, and then there were big gobs of it waiting for him to bite into. Her sandwiches were minefields.

She was always supportive of him but he wasn't supportive of her. When he was on his way to make his first speech at Toast-masters, she said to him, "So, are you excited, nervous, what?"

TJ said, "I'm nothing."

"You can't be nothing, you have to be something. Come on, what are you, really?"

"Nothing." And he left the room, his rented tuxedo flapping.

IT'S HOT IN THE apartment after the baking, so Shelley makes a piña colada for herself and a virgin one for Davis. She turns on the fan and sits in front of it with Davis beside her. She sips her drink and he spills his all over the couch.

On the flight home, Shelley didn't have any cash to buy the airplane headphones so she watched the in-flight movie with no sound. At first she thought she could make sense of it, but then a plot twist threw her for a loop and she gave up and looked out the window where there were clouds and nothing else. The other passengers were laughing and pointing at their screens. When Shelley first boarded the plane, she had surveyed their round and long and flat and fat faces, wondering if she would be stuck with them on a remote island for the rest of her life, wondering if they'd get along.

The air from the fan blows directly on Shelley and makes her hair fly around her face. She closes her eyes and pretends the breeze is an island breeze and that Davis's spilled pineapple juice is the ocean, and she wishes it is possible to steal a vacation, for real.

HER FIRST FIGHT WITH TJ had been because TJ wished one of their friends happy birthday on Facebook before she did.

"What's the problem?" TJ kept saying. "What is your problem?"

Shelley said, "You didn't even consult with me. He's my friend too."

"You only met him once."

"Even still."

"I just wrote on the guy's wall, for Christ's sake. I'm supposed to ask you before I write on somebody's wall?"

"No, but now I look like an asshole because I'm wishing him happy birthday after you. Like I didn't think of it on my own. We're supposed to be a united front. These types of things should be joint decisions, between both of us."

"You're fucked," said TJ.

IN THE MORNING, SHELLEY lies in bed next to Davis for a while and watches him sleep.

He is oblivious to everything around him. His tiny hands are curled into tiny fists and his mouth is open. His breath is warm on her face, and smells like cake.

She gets up and tries to make a swan out of her bath towel like the maid had done every day in her hotel room, but all she can manage is a flat, twisted shape that looks maybe like a snake but not even that, really. She undoes the folds and puts the towel away because she doesn't want to scare the baby. Then she packs her suitcase and calls an airport limo to take them to the airport.

She wakes up Davis by rubbing stolen sunscreen all over his moist pink limbs. When he opens his eyes, she says to him, "Let's go, my little coconut."

The limo arrives and the driver winks at them in his rearview mirror and says, "And who is this little man?"

"His name is Davis," says Shelley.

"Hello, Davis! Is this your very first trip? Where are you off to?"

Davis looks out the window and tries to get closer to the passing cars by pressing first his forehead and then this tongue against the glass.

"He's a baby," says Shelley. "He can't talk to you."

"Davis, look at me!" The driver jerks his head around and waggles his eyebrows like two bushy caterpillars.

Davis starts to cry.

Shelley glares at the driver and says "Shh" to Davis and gives him her thumb to suck, and when he stops crying and latches on, a feeling of peace washes over her like a wave.

At the airport, the two of them join one of the long lineups in Departures and move forward until there is just one family ahead of them, a mother and father and a pair of school-age kids.

The mother turns and sees Davis. "Isn't he cute."

"Thank you," says Shelley.

"I remember when mine were that small." The mother reaches out and smoothes Davis's wisps of hair.

"I guess you can't help doing that."

"What? Oh." The mother puts her hands in her pockets. "I didn't even — sorry."

"That's all right." Shelley musses Davis's hair and smiles at the woman.

A check-in clerk calls, "Next!" and the mother shuffles up to the desk with her family. The father and son and daughter are already wearing sunglasses.

EARLY IN THEIR RELATIONSHIP, TJ gave Shelley a mood necklace because he said he could never tell what mood she was in.

A mood necklace is not as effective as a mood ring because a mood ring is worn on a finger so it's touching the skin already, but a mood necklace is worn around the neck so the wearer has to hold or rub the charm to make it turn from black to blue or red or yellow. Shelley figured she'd have to have a fever or something for her charm to actually turn yellow, or any bright colour, because the brightest it ever got with her was grey.

She was playing with the necklace at the bar, where she and Monique were dancing to a song Shelley didn't recognize.

"TJ gave you that, right?" Monique sighed. "You are so lucky you have TJ."

"Yeah," said Shelley. "TJ's great."

Monique's back pocket glowed, and she pulled out her tiny phone and shrieked. "It's that guy from last week! He just texted, 'Where U at?' I'm going to tell him." She started punching keys.

A guy and a girl were grinding on the dance floor right beside them, really going at it. The girl's mouth was on the guy's neck and the guy's hands were sliding up under the girl's top.

Monique said to Shelley, "How's my tan?"

Shelley squinted at her. "It's too dark in here. I can't tell."

Monique's screen lit up again. "Oh my God, he's on his way over! I have to go to the bathroom. Be right back."

Shelley nodded, and swivelled so she was directly facing the grinding couple.

The guy had his crotch pressed against the girl from behind now. The girl was wearing a black T-shirt with a pair of glowing skeleton hands positioned so they appeared to be grabbing her breasts. Her eyes were closed, but her boyfriend's eyes were wide open. He saw Shelley watching them, and grinned at her.

She turned away fast and wrapped her arms around herself. The pink and blue strobe lights pulsed outside and the shots of coconut rum pulsed inside. She thought of TJ's hands down her pants, and was almost knocked over by the feeling of home.

When Monique came back, her lips were redder and her hair

was fluffier. "My tan is looking killer! I am going to have a serious wicked base for Cuba."

"You are such a lucky duck, Monique. I can't believe you're getting all that stuff for free."

"It's not free — it's inclusive. Maybe I'll ask that guy if he wants to be part of my package deal, ha, ha. Okay, seriously, where do you think he lives, to come all this way to see me? Do you think he's from Woodbridge, or even Pickering, maybe?"

Shelley said, "You don't know where he lives?"

SHELLEY STANDS POISED AT the front of the line, holding Davis, and then she steps sideways and starts walking across the terminal. "The thing about us," she says, "is we don't know if we're coming or going."

"Ooga," says Davis.

"Amen to that, Mister."

They get to Arrivals and Shelley finds them a couple of seats. All around them, loved ones are waiting and watching the closed doors.

"This is the best part," Shelley tells Davis, and he smears coconut snot all over his face with his little fist.

Across the room, a security guard opens his mouth and stretches his lips into a wide grin for Davis. He sticks out his tongue and rolls his eyes around. He brings his hands up and wiggles his fingers by his ears like antlers.

Shelley mushes her thumb into Davis's soft belly. "Everybody thinks you're great."

The doors slide open, and people start to file down the ramp. All of them look tired and some of them are tanned, and most of them are waving to their loved ones, and a few of them shout, "Where's a bathroom? Did you see a bathroom?" And the loved ones shout back, "Didn't you go on the plane?"

"I tried," Shelley whispers to Davis, "but they were all full."

Brave Things
that Kids Do

YOUR HAIRSTYLIST LOOKS LIKE the type of hairstylist who would listen. She looks like you could tell her anything, and she would take it all in and consider it while you were sitting in her chair that she pumps higher and higher with her foot. She always wears beautiful sandals on those feet, the kind of sandals that resemble Roman cities and you would never wear sandals like that yourself, with all of their turrets and towers and delicate beams. But she can pull them off.

She'd think about what you'd told her, and she'd snip, and then she'd say something profound like, "I believe in the beneficence of all humankind, and what you've told me shatters that belief to the core." You would watch your hair getting shorter under her scissors, which have fake jewels stuck around the finger holes, and you would feel lifted up by what she had pronounced. And you'd be high above everyone else on the pumped-up chair.

But that is actually the exact opposite of this hairstylist.

Your hair does get shorter under her scissors with the fake jewels around the finger holes, but basically she just snips away with a blank stare, and you gradually tell her less and less about your life, or anything personal at all, so by the end all you have to talk about is the weather, and the styling products you are using or would like to be using, or how much you like it when she uses the foot pump to raise the chair, because you do. She could raise and lower that chair all day, with you in it, and you wouldn't need to tell her that your longtime boyfriend of many years found someone better, and it wasn't hard either, because he only had to look as far as the girl you always knew he preferred, because she is more spontaneous than you are and because she is shaped like a stack of these things, in this descending order: apple, sideways squash, mailbox, two telephone poles, and two loaves of bread at the bottom. And you wouldn't need to tell her that there was a baby in the picture for a while but not anymore, because that is not a thing you tell a hairstylist anyway. It is enough to be here in the salon, in front of a mirror with lights all around it, and watch yourself be transformed.

ON THE WEEKEND, YOU eat birthday cake with a photo of your mother's face printed onto the icing. You get the piece with your mother's eyes on it, and they stare at you all the way up to your mouth.

Mothers are everywhere these days — on the cake, across the table from you looking concerned. The other day you ate your lunch in the park, and a parade of mothers pushing strollers lunged and squatted past you on the sidewalk, following a tiny elastic woman in camouflage spandex who shouted at them, "Kick yourselves in the butt, ladies!"

Your own mother says, "Are you doing okay?"

You push an envelope onto her placemat and she opens it and reads the card, which says, "Moms are like oven mitts. They protect you from the elements." There is a cartoon oven mitt with a smiling lipstick mouth on it.

"I got it at the dollar store," you tell her.

"YOU DON'T CELEBRATE ME," you say to your former best friend in the waiting room, but she is reading a magazine and she isn't your former best friend anyway. The only magazines in the waiting room are parenting magazines, and you have already flipped through most of them because sometimes there are the articles about how Mommy and Daddy can set some time aside from Baby to renew their own special connection, or else how Mommy can set time aside from Baby to reconnect with herself and take a scented bath or read a parenting magazine or whatever.

"You don't celebrate me," you say again, and this time the man a few chairs away, who keeps getting up to pump the hand sanitizer, looks over, and you wonder if he can see right through your skin to the five big glasses of water sloshing around inside you.

You are practising because this statement is what you are going to tell your former best friend. It has been building in you for a long time and you considered writing everything down in an email but that wasn't good enough. Then you dreamed that you had a big fight with her but then you made up, although the process of reconciliation was long and drawn out, and you were in high school again and you made endless plodding walks through the snow to get to your friend's childhood home. When you arrived, her mother and father and sister said, "It's been so long since we've seen you! What have you been doing with yourself?" And you had nothing to tell them.

You say, "You don't celebrate me." And in your mind, your former best friend says, "I don't know what you're talking about."

The receptionist calls someone's name, and the woman who is not your former best friend puts down her magazine and stands up.

"Because all of our lives you have been there for me when something bad happens. You hold my hand and you say, 'There, there,' and you tell me to cry if I have to. But when something good happens, you don't celebrate me."

You have to practise this or it will not go the way you want it to.

THE NEAT LITTLE SIGN inside the cubbyhole where you change into the purple gown that opens at the back says, in four different languages, "Please put your valuables in the plastic bin and keep it with you at all times. We are not responsible for lost or stolen items."

Then the ultrasound technician escorts you into a dark room and says, "Please lie down on the table," followed by, "When was the date of your last period?"

You say, "That's not what I'm here for."

She frowns and consults her sheet. "Oh yes," she says, and squeezes the cold jelly onto your skin. Once this part is over she tells you, "Now please empty your bladder and remove your underwear."

In the bathroom that opens onto the examining room, a small dish of potpourri decorates the toilet tank lid, and it smells like an orchard you once visited with your former best friend. When you climb back onto the table, the technician pushes a hard cushion under you and the paper crinkles under your feet.

She points to the long, blunt wand attached to the machine next to the table — "Do you know what this is for?" And you nod because you have done this before, and really what other purpose would a thing like that have?

"Now just relax," the technician says, and slides a condom onto the wand and slides the wand into you, and she hums to herself. Each time she types on the keyboard with her other hand, there is a musical bleep.

You close your eyes and listen to the radio, where the morning-show host who is back from a leave of absence is talking about his dead wife.

"Because my wife died, you see, and so I am now much more aware of the ramifications of death, and how they reach out their dark tendrils to tickle those of us who are still living. It is not so much like zombies or the undead that I am talking about here, but just the living-on of the dead in the minds of those still alive, whom they have left behind. And I will tell you another thing — it's cold outside! Here's Bill with the weather. Bill, what have you got for us? Give us some good news!"

"Thank you, Sammy. We're very happy to have you back."

"I'm very happy to be back, Bill, and thank you for saying that. Everyone at the station has been so kind. Now that my wife is no longer here with us, I am truly glad to be back among all of my co-workers who are brimming with life, and with brand-new babies and such. Like your little Alexander for example, who came out whole and perfect, a perfect baby. It's very rewarding to be welcomed back by arms thrown wide open by you, my colleagues, who are not grieving a loss such as I am. Now, how about those rain clouds — is there a silver lining for us?"

"That's a good one, Sammy. Well, we do have a cold front moving in, and we're going to get about five millimetres —"

"Let me tell you something wonderful that happened to me this morning. I went into the staff washroom, you know the one. And do you know what I saw? Ask me."

"What did you see, Sammy?"

"I saw the tiniest moth, no bigger than the nail on my pinkie finger. This moth was clinging to the grout between the tiles, and seeing it buoyed me up and gave me new hope for the future. For all of our futures. Yours and mine and little Alexander's, all of them."

The wand slides out and you open your eyes, and the technician is smiling at you.

"It's perfect," she says. "There's nothing left."

THE WAY YOU FEEL when you are sitting and talking to your former best friend, in this nice café, it's like — well, you don't know what it's like, but you do not enjoy it. She looks across the table at you and says, "So how is your art coming along?"

You say, "It's going okay."

And your former best friend could leave it there, and you'd be fine, and maybe you would go on to talk about the really incredible muffin you're eating. Because it is amazing, this muffin.

It is dense and moist and the carrots in it have been shredded almost to the point of not being an ingredient at all.

You have already talked about her art, and about people who you both know in different ways, including a few curators who work in the big galleries. She knows these curators very well; she has had dinner with them, at their houses, whereas, you say, "Yes, I've talked to them a few times but not about anything, you know, personal."

Now she leans closer and squints, and for a second you think she might compliment you on your new haircut but instead she says, "So what are you working on, exactly?"

And you want to say that you are working on erasing the memory of her, but instead you say, "It's still in the early stages."

"Did you hear about Elba?" she asks you. And you haven't, so she tells the story — you know who this woman is, used to see her at art openings, and everybody thought she was fantastic. She was even sort of famous because she knew how to operate one of those old-fashioned looms, and she made a business out of it, both by making fabric on the loom and by giving lessons on how to operate the loom. She always had people crowded around her at art openings, because let's face it, she was a true craftsperson.

But then Elba had a stillborn baby, your former best friend tells you, and instead of, say, turning the experience into something meaningful by making it into art, such as the woman could have bought a baby doll, one of those very lifelike ones, and spun a cocoon-like structure around the doll with her loom, as if to represent the baby being in a pupa, something far-out but ultimately meaningful like that, she just stopped going to art openings and stayed home all the time. And eventually when she started coming around again, all she wanted to talk about was her dead baby. And come on, if you're not going to translate that event into a narrative that people can understand, or even that people have trouble understanding but then they can at least refer to the artist's statement, then where is the value in life's sad times? You can come out on the other side of them and your suffering is bound up in the art that the sad thing inspires. But if you're not even going to do that, then you can't blame other people for eventually running out of things to say, and that's why you end up all by yourself in the far corner of the room, even though that's where the complimentary hummus and fennel sticks are — because that's how uncomfortable you make other people feel.

You think that maybe you're ready to leave the café now, so you stand up and start to walk towards the door, but your former best friend hisses, "Come back here." And the table flies across the room because it is a magic table, and you both fall onto the floor, which is covered with the apples that you picked as children from a tree that towered above you the way a sky-scraper is big.

You roll away from her, and she kicks her feet in the air and snorts, "Get over here, now!" and you don't want to because you are not her friend, not anymore, even though she is sincere in her facial features, and you once compared the mole on her neck to an actual mole because it is brown and has ears.

So you stay where you are because she is making those hissing and snorting noises, when all she has to do is say, "It's me. I'm here and you're there and people are turning around in their seats to look at us and the only thing in the world I want is the comfort of you sitting beside me." That is all she would have to say to you, and you'd go over.

But instead she tells you that if you speak with confidence there is a much greater chance that people will believe what it is you are saying. And when she opens her mouth, you see tiny fetuses or embryos or zygotes inside, and their miniature hearts are beating in pulses, which does not bestow confidence on her words. If anything it makes her words more vulnerable, because you think that in most accepted definitions of fetuses or embryos or zygotes you will find the word "vulnerable." The thing and the word are the same — the partially formed human person and its ability to be crushed between a forefinger and thumb, its state of utter dependence, the constant possibility of its being squished or otherwise snuffed out in some equally red and messy and clumpy and clotted way.

So you don't believe her, generally, when she tells you anything. This is why she is your former best friend.

IN THE WAITING ROOM before they called your name, you picked up a parenting magazine and opened it to a column on how kids can be so smart and brave, they do things such as dial 911 if their father is choking or they kick and scream for help if a stranger tries to take them. Or they curl up into a ball and hide in the back of the store if the fire alarm goes off, which hey, you don't think is so smart. That kid is going to burn, hiding like that.

Then the door opened and a little girl came in holding her mother's hand, and you wondered if this girl would ever be called upon to save a life, and if she was, would she succeed or would she fail? Because of course it could go either way. The mother let go of the girl and walked to the counter and the girl looked around at everyone in the waiting room. Then she scowled at them and raised her arms over her head and puffed out her belly and yelled, "I am a teenager!" She was only about five or six, but you believed her.

If you had a child, your child would tell you, "You should stop wasting your time, Mom." Your child would tell you to take responsibility for your own life and your own happiness, and to cultivate healthy relationships and to not watch so much TV and to maybe even reconnect with yourself once in a while. And you would listen. But not everyone can be so wise so young.

Some Wife

ON WEDNESDAY AFTERNOON, STU stopped in front of Frank's computer screen and said, "Whoa-ho! Who is that?"

"Back off, Stu-dog," said Graham from the next desk over. "That's his wife."

"That's your wife?" Stu stared. "You got good taste, Frank."

"Yeah, thanks Stu." Frank shuffled his mouse, and the photo of the tall, smiling woman in the gold bikini disappeared.

"C'mon, Frank," said Stu. "Let's see that again. That's some wife you got there."

Frank leaned back, and raised an eyebrow. "Yeah?"

"Yeah!"

"Sure, why not." Frank smiled a little, and clicked on the attachment again. "Bonnie sent me the picture this morning."

"You got a pool, Frank?" said Graham.

"Nah, that's our neighbours'. They let her use it last summer."

The pool was an impossible blue behind Bonnie in her shiny

bathing suit. She was posed with her arms arched over her head as if she were about to dive.

"Yeah!" said Stu. "All right!" Then he made a rude hip-pumping motion in Bonnie's direction and that was enough for Frank.

"Show's over," he said, not smiling anymore.

On top of Frank's monitor was one of those little puff-balls with googly eyes stuck onto it and flat plastic feet on the bottom. A small paper tag attached to the feet read, "I love you!" Stu thought about those three simple words and then he thought about the pencil case that his girlfriend Faye had given him for Thanksgiving. First of all, he didn't have a present for her because it was Thanksgiving. Second of all, she gave him a pencil case. Shaped like a dog.

He had said to her, "You want me to use this?"

"It's for work!" she said. "For your desk. To personalize it. You told me they call you 'Stu-dog' sometimes."

"I don't use pencils at work."

"But look — you unzip him and then you reach in to get what you need." Faye pulled the zipper down, opening up the toy animal's back to reveal the gaping hole inside.

"Sorry, Frank." Stu cleared his throat. "She's just, you know. She's some wife."

"He married her, didn't he?" said Graham.

"Yeah, I guess he did. Lucky guy."

"I should get back to work." Frank pulled his chair toward his desk and minimized Bonnie's email.

"Right." Stu nodded slowly. "Me too. I got a pile you wouldn't believe."

"Better get at it then, Stu-dog," said Graham.

"Yeah," said Frank, "you'd better."

STU WENT BACK TO his desk and sat down. He thought about Bonnie. He looked at his in-tray. There was a lot of stuff in there. He thought about Bonnie some more. He opened his drawer and took out some mints, which he had been saving for a special occasion. Bonnie in her gold bikini. He ate the mints.

AFTER WORK, STU WENT home and ate TV dinners with Faye.

Faye was nice, but she had a set of teeth on her that Stu had never really been able to get past. They'd been fine enough when he'd picked her up in the wine bar a few months back, where it was dark and he'd been full of Shiraz. But then the next morning — those teeth.

"Anything good happen at work?" said Faye. She'd eaten all of her food already.

"Not really." Stu glanced up from his half-finished Salisbury steak. "You have some corn on your face."

"I do?" She swatted at her mouth, and a couple of kernels fell onto her empty plate. "Oh."

"Good dinners," said Stu. But he didn't really mean it.

"Thanks," Faye said, looking at the corn.

ON THURSDAY, WHEN STU walked by Frank's desk for the fifth or sixth time, Frank started to look pissed off.

"Hey, Stu-dog," said Graham. "What is this, a peep-show?"

Stu's face got hot. "What do you mean?"

"You keep on looking at the guy's computer."

"I deleted the email," said Frank. "She's gone."

"See what you made him do?" said Graham.

"Hello, gentlemen," said a woman's voice.

They all looked over and there was Juanita, from the Festivities Committee. She smiled at them as she taped up a flyer on the wall across from Frank's cube. The flyer was printed on green paper, and had snowmen on it.

"You're all coming to the holiday party on Friday, I hope," she said.

"I hate Christmas parties," said Graham.

"It's not a Christmas party." Juanita smoothed out the flyer with both hands. "It's called a holiday party."

"Are we allowed to bring guests?" asked Stu.

"You're allowed to bring one guest. I'll be passing around a list and there's a special column on it that says, 'Guest', which you have to check off if you're bringing someone from outside the company."

"Great." Stu looked at Frank. "Did you hear that, Frank? There's a special column."

"I heard," said Frank.

"That's one guest per employee," said Juanita, "or else there's a fee."

"I hate holiday parties," said Graham.

"WHAT ARE YOU DOING over there?" Faye asked in bed that night.

Stu had rolled away from her to think of Bonnie, and snowmen. "Nothing."

"Because I'm over here." Faye leaned toward him and propped herself up on an elbow. She looked pretty uncomfortable like that.

He glanced at her. "Is that a new nightgown?"

"It's my regular nightgown," she said. "I always wear it. Don't you like it?"

"I didn't say anything about liking it or not liking it. I just asked if it was new."

She frowned a little, then brightened. She edged closer, her elbow still jammed into the mattress.

Stu stayed where he was and bunched up the covers over his lower half so Faye wouldn't get the wrong idea.

Faye said, "I'll give you a kiss if you can read my mind right now." Then her elbow gave out and she flopped sideways into the space between their pillows.

Stu closed his eyes. "I'm tired, Faye."

"YOU WEARING THAT TO the Christmas party?" Stu asked Graham the next day.

"I'm not going." Graham looked from his own Casual Fridays jeans and golf shirt to Stu's suit and tie. "Why would I go? And I don't have a guest."

"You don't have to bring one."

"You bringing Faye?"

"I'm not sure."

"Won't she be pissed if you don't invite her?"

"She doesn't know about it." Stu nodded at Frank's empty desk. "Is he going?"

"I think so."

"Did you see if he checked off the column?"

"You better watch it," said Graham.

JUANITA GAVE STU A name tag on his way into the motel ballroom that night. "Where's Faye? I noticed you didn't check off the column for her."

Stu put on a sad face. "She's sick."

"Poor thing."

He nodded, eyeing the rows of name tags waiting to be claimed.

"She's really missing out." Juanita shook her head. "There's a buffet in there like you wouldn't believe. If you don't try the pasta salad, you will regret it for the rest of your life."

INSIDE THE BALLROOM, IT was all fake snow and "Silent Night" on the P.A. system.

Stu took everything in. He saw the buffet, and he saw Frank and Bonnie standing under the glowing angel, beside the nativity display.

He pretended at first as if he hadn't seen them, and took his time making up a plate from the dishes along the food table.

Bonnie was wearing a green dress.

Stu reached for the pasta-salad spoon and closed his eyes mid-scoop. Bonnie posing by the pool in her gold swimsuit. He opened them. Bonnie standing next to Frank and Mary and Joseph in her green dress.

He ate slowly, then wiped his mouth with a reindeer napkin, threw out his garbage, and walked over to Frank and Bonnie. "Hi, Frank." He smiled.

"Hi, Stu." Frank didn't smile back.

"They really did a nice job with the decorations in here." Stu looked at Bonnie. "A real winter wonderland."

"It's all right," said Frank.

"Hi, Bonnie," said Stu. "That's a very nice dress."

Bonnie looked at Frank. "Who's this?"

"I'm Stu," said Stu. "I work with Frank."

"Yeah?" She looked at something behind him and squished her lips together.

Stu noticed they were nice, red lips; not purple or brown like Faye always had. "You tried the pasta salad yet?" he asked her. "It's got spirals."

"It's entirely possible." Bonnie blinked at whatever she was squishing her nice lips at.

"No, it's definitely got spirals. I had some."

She frowned a little, and finally looked at him. "No, I mean that I tried it. That's the possibility. There's lots of things on the buffet."

Stu puffed up a bit. "Yeah, you're right. There's lots."

"You want to move over there, Bonnie?" said Frank.

"Sure," she said. "I don't care."

"Nice to meet you, Bonnie." Stu stuck out his hand.

She stared at it for a moment, then shook it. Bonnie's hand around his. Bonnie in her green dress. She looked at him one more time before she and Frank walked away, and Stu thought he could stand there forever.

"DO YOU THINK THAT the stars get married so much because they can afford it?" Faye asked when Stu got home.

She was sitting on the couch and reading one of her glossy newspapers. "Like this — all these weddings." She had it open to a spread on Hollywood couples.

"Sure," said Stu. "I don't care."

"But stars get married a lot. I mean the same stars get married to lots of different people. And some of them marry other stars and some of them marry regular people. Why do you think that is?"

"I'm tired, Faye."

"Oh." She looked down at all the white dresses. "I was just wondering, that's all."

"Well, I can't help you there," Stu said, and left the room.

"DID BONNIE HAVE A good time at the party?" Stu asked Frank on Monday.

Frank shrugged. He didn't look away from his computer.

"She looked like she was having a good time."

"Maybe you should back off on the Bonnie talk," said Graham. "Maybe he doesn't like you making so many inquiries after his wife. Bonnie's his wife, you know."

"I know that," said Stu. "People ask about other people's wives all the time. It's not a big deal."

"Maybe you should go back to your desk," said Frank.

"Yeah, go back to your desk, Stu-dog," said Graham.

Stu stuck his hands in his pockets. "What'd you do on Friday night, Graham?"

"I didn't stare at some other guy's wife, I know that much."

"Yeah," said Stu. "Well, I got some work waiting for me. See you guys later."

"See you," said Graham.

Frank didn't say anything.

THAT NIGHT, STU CROUCHED outside Frank and Bonnie's living-room window and looked in.

Bonnie was in there, stretched out on the couch reading the paper. A real paper, with real news about real people.

Frank was not in the room.

Bonnie's lips moved as she read. *Those red lips*, thought Stu. *With nice teeth under them.* She turned a page, and the paper rose and fell with the lightest touch of her long fingers.

Bonnie was barefoot in a pair of jeans and a loose-fitting white shirt. She looked comfortable and elegant at the same time.

He wondered if she drank tea, and if she did, how she took it. He'd bring her a cup the way she liked it while she read her paper in her stylish casual clothing. They'd never eat TV dinners. They'd go to fancy places every night, and she would try on different dresses for him in their bedroom before they hit the restaurant, and maybe when she was between dresses he'd say to her, "I like that one." And she'd say, "I'm not wearing anything!" And he'd wink and say, "I know." They'd both laugh. Or maybe they wouldn't get to the restaurant at all — they'd order in, but it would still be fancy food; something with garnishes, and halfway through she'd say, "Oh, I'm full." She'd always get full halfway through.

Bonnie put down her newspaper and glanced toward the window.

Stu ducked. He sat in the snow for a few long seconds, with his heart beating fast and his pants getting wet and cold. Then, slowly, he raised his head over the sill.

Bonnie was still looking in Stu's direction, but not at Stu. She was smiling at the reflection of the man standing in the doorway, who was holding a camera in front of his face. She said something to him, and unbuttoned her blouse.

Stu pressed the fingertips of one hand against the cold window, and the flash went off.

The man put the camera down and grinned. The man was not Frank.

Bonnie said something else, and stood up. Her white blouse gaped open, showing the pink skin underneath. And her bra, which was lacy.

The man who was not Frank walked into the room. He said something and Bonnie laughed, and he grabbed her from behind and put his mouth on her neck, and then the glass between her and Stu fogged over with his rushed breath.

FAYE WAS SLEEPING WHEN Stu got home.

On her bedside table was a plate with four English-muffin halves topped with bacon slices and congealed cheese.

He lifted the covers and slipped in beside her, moved closer until his chest was pressed against her back. He put his mouth on her neck.

Faye mumbled, "I made us bacon bunnies but they got cold."

"That's okay," Stu said, and slid his hand under her nightgown.

She giggled, and flipped over so she was looking at him. Her big, uneven teeth glowed in the moonlight.

"Turn around," Stu said in a rough voice, and pushed her face into the pillow.

THE NEXT DAY, STU walked by Frank's desk to say hello.

Frank didn't say hello back. He was staring at a spreadsheet on his screen.

"You and Bonnie get up to anything exciting last night?" Stu asked him.

"I was out."

"Faye and I had a romantic evening at home. It was nice."

Frank glanced up at him. "I'm busy here."

A scrawny, fake Christmas tree was set up in the aisle next to Frank's cube. Stu reached over and squeezed one of the branches, fingering the individual plastic needles. The ornamental candy canes and silver balls shook slightly. "You two doing anything for the holidays?"

Graham leaned over. "The guy said he's busy, Stu-dog."

"I'm just making conversation," said Stu. "What about you — any holiday plans?"

"Trying not to kill myself," said Graham.

THAT NIGHT, STU WENT back to Frank and Bonnie's house.

Bonnie was reading in the living room again. This time she had a book. She was wearing a flowing, pink robe, possibly silk. Definitely not a nightgown.

Frank was not with her again.

Stu closed his eyes, and he was at their favourite table in their favourite restaurant, where the waiters made origami doves out of the napkins. He was crying because knew it was over between them, because Bonnie was supposed to be there and she wasn't. She was inside Frank's living room instead.

The last time they'd been at the restaurant together, she had told him, "I saw this documentary where people talked about their favourite things. Some people talked about their favourite travel destinations, or their favourite foods. One man said his favourite thing was his wife, and one woman said her favourite thing was her husband. But these two people were not married to each other. They were married to other people off camera, who were not interviewed." And Stu knew there was a code in there for him somewhere, but he didn't pay attention because all he'd thought at the time was how much he loved it that Bonnie watched documentaries.

They'd both ordered the chocolate mousse for dessert and it had been very disappointing. The menu said it would be deep and dark and richer than dreams, and it wasn't any of those things. It was the worst mousse they'd ever tasted, and Bonnie had said, "There's no mouth-feel to this. I'm not getting any mouth-feel here at all." And when he saw his upside-down sad face, he should've known what was coming, but he didn't. Because it was only the reflection in his dirty spoon and it didn't seem important at the time.

Stu heard a noise behind him but he didn't turn around.

Inside, Bonnie and her lips kept on reading.

"What are you doing out here, Stu?" said Frank.

Stu jerked a little at the sound, but then he pretended he hadn't heard it.

"What the hell are you doing out here?"

"Nothing," said Stu, with his back to Bonnie's husband. "I'm not doing anything."

"Turn around," said Frank. "Turn around and stop looking at my wife."

Stu turned around, and stood up slowly. "You showed us the email."

Frank curled his hands into fists. "What?"

"I'm just saying."

"I could kill you for this. I could kill you for being here outside my house and looking in at my wife and people wouldn't blame me."

Stu shuffled his feet in the snow. "Go ahead, then."

Frank stood up straighter, and let his hands fall to his sides. "I will if you ever come here again. I'll kill you if that happens."

"I won't," said Stu. "I won't ever come here again."

"That's good," said Frank.

"Okay," said Stu.

They stared at each other for a moment.

"See you tomorrow, then," said Stu.

Frank nodded. "See you tomorrow."

Todd and Belinda Rivers
of 780 Strathcona

TAMMY AND BRUCE MAKE a point of not taking each other for granted. To keep their spark alive, they go on monthly "dates," which they chuckle about because they are married, after all. They also do their grocery shopping together, but this Friday night Tammy is grocery shopping by herself because Bruce is out with his friend Gary watching the game at He Shoots He Scores, which Tammy thinks is a sexist name for a sports bar, but she doesn't like sports bars so who is she to complain?

"Are you sure you want to go by yourself?" Bruce had said to her in his thoughtful way before heading out. "We can go together tomorrow night."

"No, no, it's fine," Tammy had told him. "We need milk, and we need the pizza ingredients. We'll have fun making the pizza together tomorrow night."

"You're right," he'd said, and left.

So Tammy goes to Foodland by herself and reaches for a basket but then pulls her hand back, and decides in that moment to get a cart instead. The aisles in this store are narrow, and she and Bruce always use baskets so they don't take up too much room, but tonight she thinks, *I will get a cart. It's only me, after all.*

She yanks one out of the line and heads for the mushrooms, and it's at this point that she sees the magazine. It's lying on the bottom of the cart, with Nicole Kidman's face smiling up at her.

Tammy likes Nicole Kidman, all that frizzy red hair she has. She liked her better when you could still hear her Australian accent, but Nicole's come a long way since then. She reaches for the magazine — it's a *People* — and stops. *I should really do the shopping first*, she thinks.

She drops a few handfuls of bumpy mushrooms into a bag. She picks up a green pepper, a red pepper, and two semi-ripe tomatoes. She hasn't put anything in the main part of the cart yet, only the child-seat part, which is kind of funny because the main part has so much space, and the child-seat part has those big leg holes that things can easily fall through. She looks at Nicole Kidman again. *I'll just read the cover*, she thinks.

Tammy isn't a big magazine reader, but she will thumb through a *People* while she's waiting at the checkout. She gets a kick out of the photos of the stars in bad outfits. Not that she cares about that sort of thing — she would never actually buy a *People*. But maybe she'll take a peek while she's doing her shopping. That way she'll feel less rushed than when she's next in line and has to unload the groceries onto the conveyor belt, which is normally Bruce's job. But Bruce isn't here.

So Tammy stops the cart in the most unobtrusive spot she can find, by the cabbage — because who buys cabbage? — and picks up the magazine. And that's when she sees the address label on it, and realizes that this crisp, shiny *People* is not from the grocery store. It's from somebody's house.

"Tammy!"

Tammy jerks her head up and hugs the magazine to her chest. It's Voula.

"Hi, Voula," says Tammy.

"Fancy seeing you here!" says Voula, because Voula is always saying things like that.

"Hi, Voula," Tammy says again, because there's nothing else she really feels like saying to her.

"What have you got there? A *People*! Is that the current issue? Can I see it?" Voula thrusts an arm at Tammy's chest.

Tammy shakes her head. She takes a step back and her elbow nudges the cabbage pyramid, which teeters. She is about to say, *It isn't mine*, but instead she says, "It's not the current issue."

"But Nicole Kidman is on the current issue."

"It is Nicole Kidman." Tammy chooses her words carefully. "But it's not the current Nicole Kidman."

"Right," says Voula. "Fine, Tammy, if you don't want to let me see your *People*, suit yourself. I'm busy shopping for a party anyway. Stavros and I are having a party. We're doing a selection of meat and an assortment of cheeses. And wine. You've never seen so much wine!"

"That sounds nice," says Tammy, still clutching the *People* that doesn't belong to her.

Voula frowns and reaches past Tammy for a cabbage, which she yanks with both hands from the bottom of the pile. The rest of them tumble over each other like green and purple bowling balls and fall in a heap around Tammy's legs. Then Voula says, "Where's Bruce tonight, Tammy?"

"He's out." Tammy sidesteps a stock boy who is rushing at her, and almost trips over one of the cabbages. "When's your party, Voula?"

"Tomorrow night. And I need lots of cheese and meat because it's going to be a big party, with tons of people. So I'd better get shopping."

"Okay," says Tammy. "I'll see you later, Voula."

But Voula has already turned away from her to order some mortadella.

A CAN OF PINEAPPLE tidbits, a can of pizza sauce, a bag of pre-shredded mozzarella, and a carton of milk later, Tammy is home with the magazine. She puts away the groceries while the *People* lies on the kitchen table. By the time she'd reached the cash register, she'd read the cover and the table of contents, but that's as far as she's gotten.

The fact that this *People* belongs to Todd and Belinda Rivers of 780 Strathcona Drive hasn't really sunk in yet. She knows it belongs to them; she just hasn't let herself think too hard about it. She looks at Nicole Kidman. Nicole Kidman looks back at her. *Belinda is a nice name*, thinks Tammy. *Todd, not so much.*

The phone rings, and Tammy picks up the cordless. "Hello?"

"It's Bruce," says Bruce. "Is Tammy there?"

"It's me," says Tammy.

"Hey," he says, "you're supposed to say, 'Who's Tammy?'" Because that's their thing.

"All right. Who's Tammy?"

Bruce sighs. "It's wrecked now."

He tells her he's on his way home, and they both say I love you, and then Tammy hangs up the phone and picks up the *People*. She turns it over and turns it over again. *Todd and Belinda's*, she thinks.

There is a red mark on her leg from the cabbages, which will probably turn into a bruise. She wonders if Bruce will ask her about it.

"780 STRATHCONA IS RIGHT across the park," Bruce says the next morning. "You can walk it over to them."

It's Saturday and they are lying in bed, and Tammy has just told him about the *People*. "I guess I could."

"I'll go with you. It'll be nice."

"Nice," she says. What she's thinking is, *But I haven't read it yet.*

"Ahhh!" Bruce stretches and sits up. "So that's one thing. What else are we going to do today?"

Tammy continues to lie there. "I don't know."

"I'm going to make eggs," he says, and walks out of the room.

Tammy looks up at the ceiling, then turns her head to look out the window. The sun is bright and birds are chirping. *I'm not going to get up yet*, she thinks. *Bruce may be up and that's fine for him but I need a few more minutes of lying here.* She wiggles her feet and feels a slight breeze. Bruce has kicked the sheet loose again, and she will have to re-tuck it.

"Tammy?" Bruce calls. "Do you want scrambled?"

"Yes, please!" she calls back. Then she thinks, *No, fried.* She opens her mouth and closes it again. Scrambled will be good.

She wishes she'd brought the *People* into the bedroom but it's still on the kitchen table. She wonders if Bruce is leafing through it right now. If he's looking at Nicole Kidman and her Alsatians, which is what the article is about. "Bruce?"

No answer. *He's engrossed*, she thinks. She gets out of bed and walks down the hall to the kitchen, where Bruce is standing at the stove with his back to her. The *People* is on the table, exactly where she left it last night.

"Can you make me fried instead?" she asks.

"It's already done." He turns around with the skillet, which is full of yellow lumps. "They're already scrambled."

They sit down at the table, with the *People* between them, and eat.

"I ran into Voula at the grocery store," says Tammy. "She and Stavros are having a party tonight, with lots of cheese and meat and wine."

"I thought we were making pizza," says Bruce.

"We are. We weren't invited."

He puts down his fork. There is a tiny speck of scrambled egg on his chin. "Did she say we're not invited?"

"Well, no." Tammy gestures at her own chin, pretending to wipe it, but Bruce doesn't get the message. "She intimated it."

"But they're our neighbours."

"They live all the way across the park."

"Hey!" Bruce tilts his head and the egg morsel falls off his chin and onto the floor. "So do the Riverses!"

She frowns. "Who are the Riverses?"

"Todd and Belinda!" He points to the magazine. "Maybe they'll be there."

"Oh, right." She opens the *People* to the Kidman spread. *Her Alsatians are magnificent*, thinks Tammy.

"We could crash it," says Bruce. "The magazine will be our ticket in!"

"So now you want to go to their party? I thought we were making pizza. And I thought you didn't like Stavros."

"I don't. But you said there'd be food."

"We'll be full from the pizza."

"Then maybe we should make the pizza another night."

"But I bought the ingredients."

"Sunday," says Bruce. "We'll make the pizza on Sunday."

THEY HAVE SEX AFTER the eggs, and it's pretty good. When they're finished, Bruce says, "So what else can we do today?"

"I thought we were going for a walk," says Tammy.

"We don't need to now. We're bringing the magazine to the party, remember? So what else?"

She wants to say, *I think I'd like to do some reading.* Instead she says, "I don't know. What do you want to do?"

"We could go to the hardware store."

"What do you need at the hardware store?"

"*We* need a couple of washers and a smoke-alarm battery. And you've been talking about shelf paper, so we can get some of that too."

"Hold on," says Tammy. "I have never talked about shelf paper."

"If it wasn't you then who was it?"

"I don't know," she says, "but I have never."

"Hey," he says, "where's that bruise on your leg from?"

THEY GO TO THE hardware store. Bruce buys two washers, a D battery, and cornflower-blue shelf paper, and chats up the girl at the cash. "Since when does corn have flowers?" he says to her.

The girl laughs uproariously. She's a teenager with spiky hair and thick leather bracelets with silver studs, like dog collars. "I don't know!"

Tammy wants to say, *Corn is a flowering plant,* but all she says is, "Let's go, Bruce."

"What a nice kid," Bruce says when they're outside in the sun. "We need more nice kids like her. Real people, you know?"

Tammy doesn't say anything but Bruce is looking at her, so she nods.

"Now what?" he says. "Want to go home and lay some shelf paper?"

BY FIVE O CLOCK, THE smoke-detector battery has been installed and safety-tested, and the shelf paper has been laid. Now Bruce is doing whatever he's doing with the washers and the bathroom sink, and Tammy is finally alone with the *People.*

She sits at the kitchen table and starts to read. *Nicole pats one of her prized Alsatians and smiles. "They're my pride and joy," she says. "They're everything to me."*

"Tammy?" Bruce calls from under the sink in their bathroom, which he sometimes jokes is a "real-life water closet!" because it's so small, and opens onto their adjoining kitchen and living room, like an actual closet. "Could you get me a glass of water?"

Tammy stops reading. She wants to say, *Why don't you drink from the faucet?* But instead she gets up and gets Bruce a glass of water.

"Thanks, Tammy," he says, after he drains the glass and hands it back to her. "What are you doing right now?"

"Just reading the *People*. There's a good article on Nicole Kidman."

"She's that actress, right? Red hair? What's she doing with herself these days?"

"I don't know yet. I haven't finished the article."

"Well, what are you standing around for? Go on and get reading! You can tell me all about it when you're done."

Which makes Tammy not really want to keep reading the article, at least not right at this moment. She turns on the TV instead.

"I thought you were going to read," Bruce calls.

She flicks through the channels and sighs. "I am." She turns off the TV. "There's nothing on, anyway."

"The black one's name is Lancelot and the brown one's name is Jack," says Kidman. "And this guy here is Sonny Bono, which always cracks me up." Tammy gazes at the glossy photo of the pink-cheeked Nicole, surrounded on all sides by her magnificent dogs, with her big ranch-style house in the background. She flips to the next page and keeps flipping. The Kidman story goes on for another five pages.

After that is the Best Dressed section, and it looks like a good one. Tammy takes the *People* over to the couch and gorges her eyes on lemon taffeta, which is apparently all the rage this year. She is about to turn the page to the Worst Dressed section, which is her favourite, when Bruce stands up and says, "Try turning on this tap, Tammy."

She's holding the magazine in such a way that it appears as if Cameron Diaz has her thumb for a face. *Wouldn't that be something*, thinks Tammy. Cameron Diaz with a big, ugly thumb instead of her small, beautiful head. Ms. Diaz's spot on the Best Dressed list might not be so assured if that were the case. Then again, if *People* were being fair, it should really only be the outfit that counts. But when did *People* ever care about being fair?

"Tammy?"

She looks up to see Bruce standing in front of her with his arms dangling at his sides, a wrench in one hand. "Oh," she says. "Sorry."

"I fixed it. I fixed the drip!"

"That's great, Bruce." She puts the *People* on the coffee table.

"You have to turn on the tap to see the difference, though."

"Okay." She follows him to their bathroom and rests her hand on their toothpaste-spotted tap handle, and turns it. "Smooth."

Bruce slaps his thigh. "What did I tell you!"

Tammy puts her hand under the cold running water, feels her skin going numb.

"Whoa, six o'clock," says Bruce. "We better get ready for that party!"

VOULA WAS RIGHT. THERE are tons of people here. Tammy stands in the middle of them, by herself.

On the other side of the room, Bruce is talking to Stavros about cheese. She knows what they're talking about because she was initially included in the conversation, but as soon as the subject of cheese came up, both men became animated and Tammy walked away. Now they're even more excited because they have moved in front of the buffet table where there is actual cheese to eat. Tammy doesn't remember Bruce ever expressing such an interest in cheese to her. And he has definitely never expressed an interest in Stavros. He hates Stavros.

What's worse, the *People* is tucked up under Bruce's arm, and every time he reaches for another hunk of aged cheddar or spiced gouda, he comes a little closer to letting it fall. She should've taken it from him. Better yet, she should've told him to leave it at home. Even better still, she should've stayed home with it herself. Voula's party is the last place she wants to be. The worst part of all is Todd and Belinda Rivers from 780 Strathcona could be here, and she wouldn't even know it.

"Tammy! Fancy seeing you here." It's Voula, in a dress.

"Hi, Voula," says Tammy.

Voula frowns at Tammy, and glances over at Stavros and Bruce. "Well, well," she says. "Thought you'd crash our little party, did you?"

"It was Bruce's idea. I wanted to make pizza."

"Did you try the mortadella?" Voula has painted her lips the exact shade of peach that clashes with every type of skin tone. "It tastes like it sounds!"

"I'm not sure what that means," says Tammy.

Voula squints across the room. "What's Bruce got under his arm?"

"Nothing, it's nothing." Tammy grabs a slab of mortadella from the meat-and-cheese table nearby — she isn't really clear which one of them it is — and takes a big bite.

Voula looks away from their husbands and gives her a wink. "Like it?"

Tammy doesn't like it, not at all. But she nods and smiles and keeps chewing.

"What did I tell you?" Voula's eyes follow every twitch and quake of Tammy's jaw.

Tammy swallows and feels tears welling up. She blinks them back. "Mmm!"

"Voula!" yells Stavros.

"Tammy!" yells Bruce.

"I guess we're being paged." Voula waves at her husband. "Be right there!"

"I, um, have to go to the bathroom," says Tammy.

"No you don't."

I hate you, Voula, Tammy wants to say. Instead she says, "You're right."

The two women make their way through the crowd to their men. Tammy sees that the *People* has slid almost completely from Bruce's grip, and, just in time, she reaches out and saves it from falling. Bruce is too engrossed in the cheese to notice.

But Voula does. "Isn't that the *People* from last night? You brought it for me!"

"We brought it," Bruce says with his mouth full, "but not for you."

"Oh," Voula says, and then, "Stavros, give me some Camembert."

Stavros carefully spreads a cracker with an even layer of Camembert and hands it to her without a word.

Tammy watches them and says, "Bruce, give me some Monterey Jack."

Bruce cuts a wedge of Monterey Jack, eats it himself, and says to their hosts, "Do you know Todd and Belinda Rivers of 780 Strathcona?"

"Know them?" says Voula. "We love them!"

"Todd's in the study with our accountant," says Stavros.

Voula points toward the kitchen. "And Belinda's in there gabbing with my masseuse!"

"Did you hear that, Tammy?" says Bruce. "They're here!"

"Bruce," says Tammy, "can I talk to you for a minute?"

"Ooh," says Voula. "Secrecy!"

"Did you invite these clowns, Voula?" Stavros waggles his elbows comically.

Voula and Tammy lock eyes as Tammy and Bruce edge away.

When they are on the opposite side of the room, Tammy whispers to Bruce, "I think I want to go home now."

"But we just got here," he says. "And there's so much cheese and meat."

"I don't feel very comfortable."

"What about the magazine? What about Todd and Belinda?"

"Screw Todd and Belinda," Tammy says, and drops the *People* before she reaches up to cover her mouth.

What I Would Say

I HAVEN'T BEEN TO a party before where they served pie, have you? But I guess that's a silly question because of course you'd know the hosts, so you've probably — anyway, it's very good pie. It takes creative people to come up with a snack idea like that.

I said to Appollonia — that's who I came with — "Would you have thought of giving out pie?" And she said, "Nope." But of course Appollonia is not creative like you and me. Which she wouldn't mind me saying, by the way. We all have our strengths and weaknesses.

Now me, I've got my chapbook. But put an equation in front of me and do you think I'd know how to solve it? Give me a break! I am a words person whereas Appollonia is a numbers person, which is a skill so many of us writers and publishers haven't mastered. On the other hand, Appollonia is not a big reader. She has a subscription to *Chatelaine*, if that tells you anything. She also watches a lot of television. Let's just say she has her shows.

By saying that, I am not saying Appollonia is a bad person. Far from it. She is kind, and holds a special place in her heart for society's cast-offs. There are simply some things she will never understand because she is Appollonia, and she is a different person from you and me. A good person, certainly. But a different person. Let's say she is mainstream, and leave it at that. I mean, she's one of my good friends, and I know her and she would not think the label "mainstream" was a negative thing.

Do you remember earlier, when "Panama" by Van Halen came on? She said to me, "Who sings this, again?" And I said, "It doesn't matter, Appollonia — they're playing it ironically." But she started bopping her head to it anyway. That's the way she is. And she says the funniest things! What was it she said the other day? She's no poet but she comes out with the greatest turns of phrase. Oh, I remember. She was talking about her work — she works in an office, as in permanently — and she was explaining how she'd stood up to her boss about switching the complimentary coffee milk from two percent to one percent. Now, I'm sorry, but if you're putting it in your coffee, you cannot tell the difference between one percent and two percent, it's impossible. If you're drinking the milk on its own, then maybe. But otherwise not in a million years. And these people were up in arms about it! So they had a meeting and Appollonia called for a vote for two percent, which she knew was the consensus, but none of her co-workers backed her up so it was her alone against the boss. And do you know what she said to me at the end of her anecdote? She said, "They hung me out to frigging hang myself." Isn't that wonderful?

I asked her once for permission to write a poem about her work life. Because it is so unpoetic, there's actually an irony at work there — ha! — that's worth writing about. And Appollonia said to me, "Sure, what the hell. Immortalize me." Isn't that perfect? The things she comes out with.

Between you and me? Appollonia has lived a terrible life.

Her parents were gypsies, which is bad enough, but while at least most gypsies are known for their flair for performance, Appollonia's gypsy parents were bookkeepers. And I'm not talking librarians, which would've been something, right? So, you know, they moved around a lot. Up until she started kindergarten, Appollonia was uprooted I can't even tell you how many times. Over and over again, suffice it to say.

But she is not a complainer. Never has been. I met her in grade one, we were in the same class, and the other kids would throw blocks at her and she wouldn't say boo. That's what first intrigued me about her, actually. She also has that voice. You must know her voice, where it always sounds like she's about to burst into tears, like "Huhhh, huhhh, huhhhn," all the time, but she's not, it's just the way she sounds.

So we became friends. I'd make up the games and she was happy to go along with whatever. And I would tell her stories on our walks home from school. Yes, I was a storyteller even then. Appollonia of course enjoyed being entertained. Our friendship grew and grew. Then we lost touch for about twenty years. She went her way and I went mine, but isn't that how it so often goes, with friends.

I bet you can guess how we found each other again! The thing of it is, I only really got on there in the first place to promote my chapbook. You must do that with your press too, I'm sure. Anyway, do you know what Appollonia said when she got in touch with me? She said, "This Internet thing is the wave of the future!" I know. Adorable.

The funny thing was, I didn't remember her at first. Her name rang a bell, but it was such a long time ago. So I looked through her friends list to see if I recognized anyone, and of course I saw you, and so many of the other guests here, and I thought, What a small, small world we live in.

Soon after that we met up for lunch and got reacquainted. I took her to that place, what's that place called. You know, the restaurant that's loud, with the salad they make from things that fall out of trees? That's where we went. And it all came rushing back to us. Grade school. Playing. Our story-time walks. And I told Appollonia about my chapbook and she said — if you can believe it — "What's a chapbook?" Oh dear. So I explained it to her, and she was thrilled for me and asked me could she buy it in the bookstores, and I said no, she could only buy it directly from me. Poor thing, she has no idea how it all works.

She doesn't know anything about the scene either, but I guess why would she? Just because she knows all these people through — how does she know all these people? She's really kept that to herself. Although she's never even heard of sp@cebar, which is amazing to me. To be that out of touch with what's going on in the world. You put out his last flipbook, didn't you? She said to me, "Well, what does he do?" And I said, "He engages with the absence of sound. He communicates his poetry through gestures and facial expressions." And she said — you'll get a real kick out of this — "Isn't that what a mime clown does?" I said to her, "Appollonia, sp@cebar is not a mime clown. He is a soundless poet." She really doesn't have a clue. I mean, I've never seen one of his performances, but at least I know, you know?

Appollonia is an accountant now, and she's married to a man named Bob who's in one of the trades, I can't remember which, and they've talked about children and they bought a condo, but not a loft condo, it's one of those postage-stamp cookie-cutter high-rise ones, which she is going to have a very hard time selling, but still, it's property and you've got to believe that owning any property in the city is an achievement these days. I said that to her too, and she said, "Do you really think it'll be hard to sell?" I told her, "Appollonia, none of us has a crystal ball." Well, maybe some of us do. Appollonia's parents might!

And Appollonia is going to be a mother herself some day. Which is the last thing I'd want to be, but who am I to judge? The second-last thing I'd want to be is a homeowner. The Appollonias of the world are welcome to it. I explained to her that renting is the way to go if you're an artist, and I told her, "Appollonia, you are so lucky you're not a creative person. You are so free!" And do you know what she said to me? She said, "Well yeah, it's true, I guess I am pretty lucky that way. None of those pesky thought bubbles overhead to weigh down my empty noggin!" I'm telling you, she says things like that all the time! It's hilarious. But of course also very sad.

The thing about me is, I think about other people. Other people are always at the forefront of my mind. And I worry about Appollonia, I really do. She's a bit of a loner, so she's not the best with crowds, which is why I said I'd come with her tonight and keep her company. Okay, I'll come clean and admit that there are people at this party who I would like to meet, of course there's that. But really I am here for Appollonia.

I wasn't even going to come over here but Appollonia said I should. One of her favourite sayings is, "Why not go out on a limb, because that's where the fruit is." Priceless, I know. That's what she said to me earlier, when I happened to mention that it might be nice to talk to you about my chapbook and about poetry in general. So here I am.

There are people who might say to me, "What are you doing with a person like Appollonia?" And I would say to those people, "Hold on, back up, please. Appollonia is my friend. Don't tell me what she's like — I know what she's like. But she is my friend who I care for very deeply." That's what I would say.

You know, I'm so glad I met you, you're so easy to talk with. And you're enjoying the pie too, I see! Oh, I'm sorry. Strudel. And here I thought it was pie all this time. Now isn't that funny, because I'm normally very observant. I can even show you right here in my chapbook, it has all these observations I make every day, transformed into verse. I've got this acrostic series on yearning, let me find that page ... You do? No, no, of course, I know how it goes. You've got people you need to — sure. It's a party! I really should be getting back to Appollonia, she's starting to look pretty lonely over there. You mean that's where you were — well, perfect, the three of us, then! Oh. Really? No, sure, I understand completely, I don't mind at all. I was on my way to the bathroom, anyway. Where is the bathroom, do you know? Of course you'd know. Could you please just point me in the right direction before you — you don't know? Well, that's fine. I'll find my way there eventually.

Our Many-Splendoured Humanity

WE'VE GOT NEIL AND Maxine over, and Neil and Maxine are not getting along, as per usual.

"That's funny," she says to him.

He frowns. "What's funny?"

"The label on that barbeque sauce."

The label on the barbeque sauce Neil is putting on his burger says, "Too Bold For Your Wife." He looks at the label. "What's funny about it?"

"It says it's too bold for me."

He takes a bite of his burger, chews. "It is."

Maxine holds the bottle upside-down over her meat and squeezes out a thick, red line. She fixes her top bun in place and looks at me. "I bet this is Deb's barbeque sauce, isn't it, Deb?"

"Oh, no." I stick up my hands. "Don't get me involved."

Marv just sits there, watching Maxine about to blow her head off with his barbeque sauce, which I never touch. I'm not one for hot things — except maybe for Marv, when we're both in the mood and the lighting is right, ha, ha.

Maxine takes a bite, and we all watch her chew.

"You like that, Maxine?" Neil says in a loud voice. He flaps his comical tie at her, which is Neil's trademark. This one's shaped like a pickle, of all things.

Maxine starts to sweat, and I go to the kitchen and get her some water.

"Gaaahhhh!" she says, and grabs the glass from me.

There's a knock on our door, hard enough to jerk our welcome mat forward a bit.

Marv squints over. "Now, who could that be?"

Neil and Maxine have a welcome mat outside their house that says, "Friends Welcome, Relatives By Appointment." Neil bought it because he said it cracked him up. One time Maxine's mother came by and rang their bell. Neil was the only one home at the time, and he peeked out the window to see who it was. When he saw his mother-in-law outside, he waved at her and pointed to the mat, and he waited until she eventually went away. Which kills me, because if Marv ever did that to my mother? Well, suffice it to say *he* would not be welcome after something like that.

Marv walks to our door and there's another knock, even harder this time. "Okay, okay," he says, and he opens up and it's our new neighbour who recently moved in down the hall from us, who we haven't really talked to yet, but we've been meaning to introduce ourselves so here's our opportunity!

"Hey, um," he says, "I just moved in down the hall?" Then he mumbles his name, so I don't catch it.

"Nice to meet you," says Marv. "I'm Marv."

I walk over and stand next to him. "And I'm Deb. Welcome to the neighbourhood!"

Marv extends his hand, and his soft arm does an eely dance with our new neighbour's nicely muscled one before their palms connect in a sort of half-shake, half-slap. "What can we do for you, neighbour?"

"Um, yeah. I was wondering if you guys have any DVDs I can borrow?"

"DVDs, eh?" says Marv. "I think that can be arranged. Come on in."

Our new neighbour grins at us and strolls into our living room, and I am almost literally blinded by the whiteness of his teeth — he could be in a commercial, they're so dazzling white, like stepping outside on a sunny winter day.

We all smile back, but I notice that Maxine's smile is kind of lopsided and I feel bad for not telling her about him earlier. But then I think I shouldn't feel bad because whenever I've seen him in the hall he's been very polite, and when he and some helpers were carrying expensive-looking stereo equipment into his apartment on the first of the month, they all seemed very friendly, and why should I have to inform people, anyway?

The thing about Neil and Maxine, though, is that they're not quite as liberal-minded as me and Marv. They're our best friends and all, but you know how it goes when you and your friends have diverse opinions on certain issues — you have to agree to disagree. As in for instance if a commercial for those poor starving African babies comes on and your friends roll their eyes and change the channel, you know that's wrong, but you don't necessarily say anything. You have to be content just knowing.

"You're doing me a real favour here," says our new neighbour. "I got my girl over with nothing to watch."

"How about watching each other?" says Neil.

"Right," says Maxine, "like you ever watch me anymore."

Neil scowls. "What's that supposed to mean?"

Our new neighbour starts going through Marv's video shelf. "Huh," he says, "you got that one. I heard that's a good one."

"What kinds of movies does your girl like?" says Neil.

He raps his knuckles on his leg. "Damn, I should've asked her that."

"Don't feel bad," says Maxine. "The most important thing is that you care."

Neil holds up the end of his pickle tie so it points in a straight line. "What's that one we watched last week, Marv? Give him that one, with the gangs."

"I was thinking more a romance," says our new neighbour.

Maxine rolls her eyes. "Oh my God, Neil, you are the biggest idiot!"

"What?" he says. "I'm making conversation."

Don't get me wrong — we love Neil and Maxine. But when it comes to things like social justice and all that, there are questions that arise such as, *What can the average person do?* and, *Can one person make a difference?* Now, if you asked me and Marv those questions, we would say yes right away. But all I'm saying is, if you asked Neil and Maxine those same questions, you might get a different answer.

For instance, a few years ago for our New Year's Eve, Marv and I volunteered at a soup kitchen downtown, which is something that Neil and Maxine have never done. I served the tables and Marv was in charge of potatoes, and we had a ball. I went in there not knowing what to expect, and I'll admit I was slightly worried, safety-wise. But I'm telling you, every one of those homeless people I gave a plate to (with the exception of a certain rumpled gentleman who complained about portion size) was so well-mannered and so grateful that frankly I was overwhelmed by a love for our many-splendoured humanity. It was a very positive experience and I'm certain that all of us went home that night feeling a little bit better about ourselves.

"I like your earrings," our new neighbour says to Maxine.

"Thank you." She blushes. "I made them myself."

Maxine is heavily into Fimo, which is jewellery you bake. Lately she's been doing desserts — her earrings tonight are two teensy blueberry pies.

"That's pretty cool," says our new neighbour. "I wish I was creative like that."

"Oh, everybody has creativity inside them," says Maxine, who, I'm relieved to see, is clearly warming up to him.

"Here." Marv hands our new neighbour a video. "This is one of Deb's."

"Right on." He looks around at our half-finished plates. "Oh, man, I'm interrupting your dinner. Sorry about that."

"No problem at all," says Marv, and I'm reminded yet again of the size of his heart. Which is very big.

Then Neil has to go and ruin everything by asking our new neighbour, "You ever tried this barbeque sauce? It's really hot, I bet you'd like it."

Maxine glares at him, and I want to hide somewhere, but thank goodness our new neighbour doesn't take offence because all he says is, "Nope. But if it's too hot for your wife, it's way too hot for me."

Maxine giggles and Neil is speechless, which is very out of character for Neil.

Marv and I wave goodbye to our new neighbour, who is now so much closer to being a friend than a stranger.

I HAVE A BAD day at work the next day because as a reward for a project I did, my boss gives me another card. On the front is a photo of a snail on a skateboard. The inside reads, "Congratulations — you're on the fast track to success!"

"Now, how do you think they found a skateboard small enough for a snail?" says my boss, Lee-Ann. "Imagine, somebody has the kind of job where they go out into the world and look for tiny little skateboards for snails, isn't that something?"

"They doctored the photo," I tell her. "That's what they do with photos now. The skateboard isn't really that small."

"You get it, right?"

"What do you mean, do I get it?" I say. "Is it a joke?"

"Of course it's a joke. Because snails are usually slow, but it's on a skateboard so that means it's going fast!" Lee-Ann throws her head back and laughs, showing her teeth. Lee-Ann's teeth look like pylons around a bad accident.

"I don't think it's supposed to be a joke," I say. "A joke has a punchline. This has a photo and some words about the photo."

"Oh, you!" says Lee-Ann.

I close the card and the two pieces of flimsy cardboard make a sound like this: *Whap*.

"SHE'S ALWAYS GIVING ME cards with backhanded compliments on them," I say to Marv over wine spritzers that night. Marv makes spritzers like nobody's business. "It's getting to be too much, I'm telling you."

He shrugs his round shoulders. "Maybe you're reading too much into them."

"No, Marv." I sip my drink. "That is not the situation here at all."

My Marv has the roundest shoulders of any man I've ever known. I tell him he's got ice-cream sundaes under his sleeves, his shoulders are so nice and round — and he says I'm the cherry on top, aww.

Knock, knock.

Marv looks at our door. "Who could that be?" He answers it and there's our new neighbour from down the hall again, with our video.

"Hi," he says to us. "I brought your DVD back."

"Did your girlfriend like it?" I ask him.

He nods, and grins. "She cried all over me."

"Glad to hear it." Marv takes the video and taps it on his leg in a thoughtful way. "She sounds like a special lady."

"She is special," says our new neighbour. "She's the best."

"How'd you meet her?" Marv asks, and I do a double take because Marv isn't usually interested in this sort of thing.

Our new neighbour half-closes his eyes. "We were at the arcade."

"Ah." Marv nods. "The arcade."

"Marv and I met on a blind date," I tell our new neighbour. "Actually, I was supposed to go out with his friend Joe, but Joe was sick that night so he sent Marv instead. Isn't that a hoot?"

"Do you have nice handwriting?" he says to me.

"Pardon?"

"Because I wrote her this poem." Our new neighbour takes a few steps into our living room, and hands me a folded-up piece of paper and a card. On the front of the card are two champagne glasses, bending towards each other. "See that?" he says. "It's like they're kissing."

Marv leans in for a peek. "Huh, will you look at that."

"They doctored this photo," I say. "Glass can't really bend that way."

The card is blank inside. I unfold the paper, and scribbled all over it are pairs of rhyming words: "unite" and "appetite", "sunshine" and "super-fine", and "mirage" and "camouflage".

"That's my poem. I was hoping you could maybe copy it down into the card? Because ladies have better handwriting than guys? So it looks nice."

"Deb's handwriting is the best," says Marv. "Her grocery lists are as fancy as invitations from the Queen."

"Thanks, Marv," I say, and I'm kind of blown away because I didn't think he noticed things like that.

Our new neighbour beams at me. "You don't mind?"

"Of course not," I say, and I close the card and it makes a sound like this: *Whutt.*

THE NEXT DAY AT work, I copy out the poem because who are we as human beings if we can't be neighbourly?

Then Lee-Ann sashays into my cubicle with a bag of St. Hubert, that French chicken with the rooster, and she has the sauce that comes with it and she's drinking the sauce right out of the container. "My husband's taking me out for our anniversary tonight," she says. "Mmm, this is good chicken sauce."

I cover up the card and the poem with one of my reports. "I prefer Swiss Chalet, myself."

"We have a coupon for the restaurant we're going to, but Ronnie said he might not even use it because it's our anniversary and we should splurge."

"That sounds decadent."

"It is decadent! That is exactly what it is." Lee-Ann smiles, and smacks her lips. "What are you and Marv doing tonight?"

"Oh," I say, "I don't know. It's not our anniversary, or anything."

"Ronnie says we should treat every day like it's our anniversary. Because what if you die and you don't get another one?"

"I have to finish this project, Lee-Ann."

"Ooh! How's it coming?" She reaches into her bag and digs around, and pulls out a wing.

I shrug. "I'm doing my best."

"I know you are, Deb," she says, and pats me on the arm with her greasy hand. "I know you are."

"SHE'S VERY PATRONIZING," I tell Marv over spritzers that night, after leftovers. "She has a real tone that she uses with me."

"Maybe if you told her how you felt," he says.

"Do you really think it's that easy, Marv?"

Knock, knock.

Marv looks at me. "Did you do the card for him?"

"Yes, I did the card for him. Sheesh, you're getting as pushy as he is."

"Shh!" Marv's eyes are wide.

"Oh, for Pete's sake," I say, and I get up and answer the door. Lo and behold, there is our new neighbour. "Hi," he says.

"Hello," I say.

He crosses his arms, uncrosses them, then lets them dangle at his sides. "So did you get a chance to —"

"Yes, yes." I hand him the card, with my neat poem. I'd thrown away his messy piece of paper. "Here you go."

He opens it, and his face lights up like a neon sign on a very dark street. "Oh, wow. She is totally gonna freak over this!"

"I put extra X's and O's at the bottom," I say, and I smile and try to catch Marv's eye, but he's looking at our new neighbour.

"Do you love her?" Marv asks him.

"What?" I say.

"I love her so much it hurts."

Marv nods. "That's what I thought."

"Oh, man." Our new neighbour glances around. "You're drinking wine. Am I interrupting a romantic moment here?"

"Well," I say.

"Nah," says Marv. "They're spritzers — you want one?" He gets up and heads to the kitchen with our empty glasses.

"Yeah? Hey, that would be great!" Our new neighbour winks at me and steps inside. "You guys are too kind."

"Aww," I say.

"Here you go." Marv walks over with three spritzers and hands one to our neighbour. "Pull up a couch, ha!"

And I have to laugh because every so often Marv can be a real riot, in his own way.

"Look at that, a lime and everything!" says our new neighbour, still standing.

"Don't mention it." Marv sits next to me on the loveseat, and we both smile and wait for our new neighbour to sit down.

"Well," he says, "my girl's waiting so I better get going."

"Oh," I say.

"Oh," says Marv.

I look at Marv and he looks at me, and I say, "We didn't realize —"

"Gotta keep her entertained, you know?" Our new neighbour grins. "I was actually wondering if I could borrow another DVD for tonight."

Marv puffs out his cheeks, but then in true Marv fashion says, "Well, sure. Why not?"

"Great." Our new neighbour goes back to Marv's video shelf and grabs something. Then he says — and this is the kicker — "Do you think you could make a spritzer for my girl too?"

"For —" says Marv, and then, "Of course." And he goes to the kitchen and makes a spritzer for this girl, who we haven't even met.

"You guys are the best." He tucks our video under one arm, next to my poem, and takes the second spritzer.

"Don't mention it," Marv says, again.

"You're gonna make a hero out of me, you know that?" Our new neighbour gives me another wink, and then he's gone.

Marv closes the door, and after a few seconds, he shakes his head and says, "Can you beat that, Deb?"

"No, Marv," I say. "No, you cannot."

"WHAT ARE THESE?" MARV asks Maxine a few nights later, when she and Neil are over again.

"Cream horns," she says. "We got them from the Greek bakery down the street."

Neil waggles his eyebrows. "I'll give you a cream horn."

"Shut up, Neil," says Maxine. "You have to try one, Marv. They melt in your mouth. Those Greeks know pastry." She fondles one of the miniature cupcakes swinging from her earlobes.

Marv peers inside the white box, at the pile of greasy cones with their pale filling. "I don't know."

"Come on, give it a go, Marv," I say. "I'll split one with you."

"All right," he says, and takes a bite.

Neil polishes off a whole horn to himself, picks his teeth with his finger, then points that same finger at Marv. "So you just gave him another spritzer, is that right?"

Marv's mouth is full, so I say, "What else was he supposed to do?"

"He could've said no. This is your apartment, is it not?"

"It's your home," says Maxine.

"He still hasn't returned our glasses," I say. "They're part of a set."

Marv swallows, frowning. "He should definitely bring those glasses back."

I hand him a napkin to wipe some cream off his chin. "The thing is, if you give someone something and they don't say thank you, that's when I start feeling uncomfortable."

"Who wouldn't feel that way?" says Neil.

"What you're describing is a very normal reaction," says Maxine.

"It's taking advantage, is what it is." Marv balls up the napkin. "Plain and simple."

Then there's a knock on our door, with a definite banging quality to it.

"What kind of person knocks on someone else's door like that?" says Maxine.

"Guess who," I say.

"Should I answer it?" Marv says to me.

I shrug. "He can probably hear us in here."

Neil smoothes his tie, which is shaped like corn on the cob. "If it's him, you should probably say no to whatever he's asking."

"Otherwise he'll keep coming back for more," says Maxine.

Marv gets up, and I can tell he's nervous because he forgets to put down his cream horn. He opens the door, and surprise, surprise, it's the new neighbour from down the hall. With his arm around some girl. "Hi there," says Marv.

"Hi," says the girl. "Here's your DVD back."

"Great." Marv takes it, and nods at her with a stiff neck. "Thank you."

"It was a good one." She's got the card in her other hand, pressed against her leg.

The new neighbour peers inside at us, smiling. "Sorry for interrupting the party, but I wanted to —"

Maxine coughs, and Neil clears his throat loudly, and I say, "Marv," and Marv says, "No," shaking his head fast. "I don't think we have anything more for you here, I'm sorry." He squares his round shoulders, and the rest of us all sit up a little straighter.

The new neighbour stops smiling, and he tightens his grip

on the girl and says, "Sure. I wanted to introduce my girl to you guys, but whatever, that's all right."

The girl frowns and tightens her grip on the card, which they haven't even thanked me for. "I thought you said they were nice," she says.

"They were." And he takes the card from her and flicks it onto the floor — how do you like that! — and the tip of it gets stuck under our welcome mat. Then the two of them turn and walk away.

Marv's shoulders fall, and he stands at the open door with our video in one hand and his half-eaten dessert in the other, looking at the empty hallway. He bends to put down the video and pick up the card, which as it turns out doesn't have champagne glasses on the cover — it's got flowers all over it. He flips it open and it doesn't make any sound at all.

"That's telling him, Marv," Neil says, and he pinches Maxine's thigh and she squeals like a teenager.

"Hey, Marv," I say, to snap him out of it. "Give me that goddamn cream horn."

Because he's just standing there, doing nothing as per usual, and it's killing me.

Unique and
Life-Changing Items

THE US PRESIDENT WAS in the news again, saying nice things about his wife. Pauline wished he would stop doing that because Dale never complimented her in public, or when they were alone either, and because the president and the first lady were making news all the time, it was hard not to compare the two relationships.

In today's paper, the president was quoted as saying, "Let me tell you about the first lady: She has arms like branches in an enchanted forest." There was a photo of him and her and the Canadian prime minister, and they were all wearing short-sleeved tops and saluting each other in an exaggerated way.

Then Dale's bare foot was on the page, wriggling. "What do you think of this coffee table, Pauline?"

She stared at the thick, black hairs on his big toe. "It's okay."

"I'm sick of it. It stinks, this coffee table."

"I don't think it stinks," she said.

"Well, it's shitty, anyway."

Pauline moved farther down the couch and unfolded the Human Faces section. There was an article about a man who had miraculously cheated death twice — the first time he had become lost in the woods and had to survive on grubs and berries until one day, he said, "a path opened up, as if someone was showing me the way home," and the second time he had fallen into the sea and would have drowned but a "very friendly" rainbow perch guided him safely to shore — and he was interviewed about how those experiences had changed his life. "It's really embarrassing," he said, "but I'm still not going to the gym regularly." Pauline reached for her pad of sticky notes and a pen.

Dale was always throwing out the newspaper and the grocery flyers before Pauline had a chance to read them, so she'd started putting sticky notes on the things she wanted to read, to stop him from throwing them away. The sticky notes said, "Please leave."

PAULINE HAD A RECURRING dream in which she was a small dog. She ran and fetched balls and sticks and she hated her leash but she wore it because her owner wanted her to, and she loved her owner. She was a female dog but she lifted her leg to pee. She ran circles around bigger dogs and was not afraid of them. She liked open fields because her owner lived in a small apartment, which is why Pauline was a small dog because that's all her owner had room for. A small dog, and an enormous armoire. Because the owner's mother had told her early on, "Buy one thing that makes you happy." And that was the armoire. Pauline would lie at her owner's feet and the owner would pet Pauline's fur with her toes while she talked on the phone to her friends, who told her, "Find one man who makes you happy." Which is why she brought Pauline home from the pet store, but then she found out she was a bitch and was disappointed.

THAT NIGHT, PAULINE AND Dale watched TV together. They sat next to each other on the couch and when the program started, Dale said, "I love this show."

And Pauline said, "I love it too."

Then they were right into the action, really in deep, and they made comments to each other like, "I can't believe he just did that!" And, "There is no way she's going to let him get away with what he just did."

"Here it comes," he said.

"He is really going to get it this time," she said.

Then a commercial came on.

It was an ad for cat food, but it wasn't a funny ad or anything, so they couldn't even laugh. And they didn't have a cat.

The cat stuck its face into a bowl and ate the food, and Dale rapped his knuckles on their coffee table. "We need a new one of these," he said.

LESS THAN A YEAR ago, Pauline went to see a play put on by a woman she'd known back in university. She ran into the woman at a bar and the woman hugged her and seemed genuinely thrilled to see her, and gave her a photocopied flyer and said, "Hey, come to my play." She sounded very sincere so Pauline went, and the play itself was nice enough — it was a one-woman show and there were parts she didn't understand because it was supposed to be postmodern, such as the part where the actress danced with a rope and then pretended that same rope was her long-lost cousin. The play was in the university woman's garage, and at the end, the actress turned on the automatic garage door opener and the garage door opened, just like that. All of a sudden there was the outside world, framed for the audience. And Pauline realized that she and the six other audience members were also framed for the outside world, in their two rows of camping chairs. And for a little while after that, a week or so maybe, nothing was the same for her. Things tasted different — she would eat an apple and it would taste more like a peach, things like that. She saw the world in a whole new light. But then everything went back to normal.

THE NEXT DAY THEY went to IKEA and walked around the show-room, which was crammed with rugs made to look like patches of grass and kids' beds shaped like caterpillars and lamps that resembled glowing fungus, and they tried not to make eye contact with any of the other couples who were doing the same thing. Some of the couples looked happier than Pauline and Dale and some of them looked unhappier.

Dale had a paper napkin full of meatballs — he'd got an extra order on their way out of the cafeteria. "What about that one?" he said with his mouth full. He had lingonberry sauce on his teeth.

Pauline looked where he was looking. The coffee table was bigger than theirs, with a darker finish. "It's all right."

"I want you to love it, though."

"I don't love it."

"Then how about that one over there?" The table he pointed to was triangular.

Pauline shook her head, and stopped in front of a cardboard television. "I like this," she said.

A small child emerged from a corrugated plastic tunnel beside them, and howled like a wolf.

"Sometimes you throw me for a loop, Pauline," said Dale. "You want a meatball?"

AFTER IKEA THEY WENT to visit Dale's ex, Sheena, in the hospital.

There was condensation in her breathing tube and the bandage over her I.V. line was curling up, but Dale said to her, "Looking good, Sheena."

"No I'm not, but you're sweet." She smiled at Pauline. "Isn't he such a suck-up?"

"Ouch," said Pauline. The two of them looked over at her and she said, "The baby kicked me."

"Oh, now that is amazing," said Sheena. "I think it's simply wonderful that you two are bringing a new life into the world."

"It's pretty cool, right?" said Dale.

A nurse walked into the room carrying a tray of pudding cups, and put one on Sheena's side table. "You're going to love this," she said. "It's butterscotch."

"Whoa, lucky!" Dale said, then, "How's she doing, Nurse?"

"Oh, we take it one day at a time here." The nurse's pale-green uniform camouflaged her against the pale-green walls, so that her head seemed to float in mid-air and her splayed feet in purple Crocs seemed to be sprouting from the floor. "But this lady is a force to be reckoned with. She keeps on going." She reorganized the pudding cups on the tray and disappeared down the hall.

"Pauline," said Sheena, "can I touch your belly?"

"It's going to blow your mind, Sheena," said Dale. "There's a party going on in there."

Pauline stepped forward, and Sheena placed her thin hand on Pauline's bulging middle. "Tell me if it kicks."

"You'll know," said Pauline.

"Did you two hear what the president said about the first lady today?" Sheena asked them. "He loves her so much!"

"You know any good places to buy a coffee table, Sheena?" said Dale. "There's nothing at IKEA."

"Oh God, I am so past IKEA. You need to go to Alphonse's. He does things with wood that are not to be believed."

Dale rubbed his hands together. "I like the sound of that!"

"Dale wants us to get a new coffee table," said Pauline. "But I think the one we have is fine."

"You need new things when you have a child." Sheena's papery lids fluttered closed, and she smiled. "Oh, and the birth! Your parents will be there, of course, waiting breathlessly to become grandparents." She opened her eyes. "Bert and Viv are going to be over the moon."

"They will be," said Dale. "You know what they're like."

"My dad already told me that he and my mom aren't driving to the hospital if it snows," said Pauline.

"But you're having the baby in February," said Sheena.

"Her father doesn't drive in the snow," said Dale.

"But it's their grandchild! Don't they want a grandchild?"

"They want a grandchild," said Pauline. "They just don't want to drive in the snow." She took a step back, and Sheena's hand dropped off her belly. "Winter driving can be dangerous."

"So, this coffee table place," said Dale. "How do we get there?"

PAULINE MET DALE DURING the tomato scare a couple of years back. Some people in the States got sick from a shipment of tomatoes from Chile, and the next thing everyone in Canada knew, they weren't putting tomatoes on the subs at the sub shop Pauline always went to.

"No tomatoes," said the sub guy.

"Are you out?" said Pauline.

He shook his head. "They're poison."

"Poison tomatoes, what will they think of next?" said the man in line behind her, who turned out to be Dale.

"I don't think anybody thought of it, exactly," she said to him.

He winked her. "That's the whole point, right there."

"We can offer you shredded carrots instead," said the sub guy.

"My wife is dying," said Dale.

"Oh my God," said Pauline, and then she said yes to the carrots.

ON THE WAY TO Alphonse's Lumber Loom, Pauline said, "I think I'd like to try out for a play."

Dale looked away from the road to her face, then down at her roundness. "What, now?"

"There might be a play with a pregnant woman in it."

"You're seriously looking for more stuff to do? You're so busy already."

Pauline spent most of her time these days on the computer, Googling things that were contraindicated in pregnancy. There were a lot of them, and if you didn't stay on top of what was bad for you, there was no telling the damage you could do.

"I think it would be nice to do something creative," she said.

"Maybe. But what if you gave birth before the play started?"

"Then I could stuff a pillow up my shirt."

"But you'll have to look after the baby then."

"You could look after him on the nights when I do the play."

Dale braked at a stoplight and grinned hugely at her. "You think it's a boy?"

A FEW MONTHS INTO their relationship, Dale started dropping hints about babies. He said things to Pauline such as, "You know what would be fun? Having a baby."

Pauline would have the newspaper spread out on the coffee table, and she'd hear Dale in the computer room watching YouTube videos of other people's infants. She heard crying, laughing, goo-gooing. She pictured a wiggling carpet of endless naked cherubs tumbling over each other and flexing their doughy limbs, their perfect miniature bums winking in the sun. The unseen parents murmured and cooed. When they weren't filming their children, they were building them sandboxes and tree houses, or stewing and blending fruits and vegetables into mush and freezing the mush in ice cube trays for portion control. They declared to their friends and relatives that they would never use disposable diapers and then conceded, "Okay, maybe just when we're travelling." Pauline listened to high-pitched squeals and chubby fingers plinking on xylophones. Dale called to her, "You have to watch this!" and "If you miss this part, you're going to regret it!" But she said she'd rather keep reading the paper, about all the senseless foreign-aid-worker deaths lately, or the recent string of brutal home invasions. "This is really life-affirming!" he shouted. There was a crash followed by more frenzied plinking, and Dale chuckled, and sighed.

About a year later, after Pauline peed on a little wand and waited two minutes and saw the cross form in the circle, she went for a walk.

Dale was at work. She could have called him, but she thought it would be more appropriate to tell him in person.

She walked through the park near their house, and it had rained so the trees were lush and dripping. Near the playground was a pack of pre-teens filming each other with a tiny movie camera.

"Take that, you fool!" one of them yelled before he jabbed his friend with a cardboard sword. They were all wearing capes or cat ears or butterfly wings, and they had drawn whiskers and sharp teeth on their faces. The kid holding the camera circled the others, his long tail swishing back and forth.

Pauline wanted to sit and watch them, but everything was wet. Her feet were soaked too — she looked down and realized she'd wandered off the path into the long grass.

"Do you surrender?" yelled a butterfly, or maybe it was a moth, and then a clap of thunder and a few drops made them all scream, and scatter.

A dog barked somewhere far away, and Pauline wondered if she had the energy to run home.

A GIANT MUSKOKA CHAIR was on display outside Alphonse's, and Pauline wanted to sit in it.

"I don't think it's safe," said Dale.

"It's just a big chair."

"But you'd have to climb."

"You could take a picture. It'll be hilarious because I'll look so small."

"Let's go inside," he said.

They went in, and Dale headed straight for the coffee tables. Pauline stood by the entrance, gazing at the vast expanse of wood creations.

There were bookshelves carved out of tree trunks with the bark still on them, cabinets made from branches and twigs, benches constructed from layers of old barn boards and antique signs, high chairs carved as ornately as thrones. And at the far end of the store, lit by a single bare bulb, was an armoire.

Dale was talking to a tall man in overalls as Pauline picked her way through the bristling, knobby furniture to the back. There was that pale light ahead of her, but somehow the store was getting darker the farther she went. She pushed her feet through drifts of sawdust and ran her fingertips along bumpy surfaces.

When she reached the armoire, she heard Dale say, "I want her to love it."

She read on the tag that the armoire was made from "a majestic cedar." She pulled out one drawer at a time, and both of them slid like they had been oiled.

"What are you looking at over there, Pauline?" Dale called.

"An armoire."

"I don't think we need one of those."

There were two little doors at the top with gleaming silver handles. She opened them and poked her head into the empty space, and was surprised by how cool it was.

"Pauline?" Dale's voice was muffled.

"We could put the baby's clothes in it," she said.

"Come and check out this coffee table. Alphonse built it to look like a giant bird's nest, it's awesome!"

She didn't move, just stood there with her cheek resting on the smooth wood.

"Don't worry, there's a flat part in the middle for drinks and stuff. There's even a spot where you can put your feet up if you want — you know how your feet get all swollen. Alphonse says a unique handcrafted item like this can totally change people's lives!"

There was a stillness inside the armoire that she liked. The part of the store she could see was so bright it made her squint. Dale and the other man moved stiffly around a giant bundle of sticks and dried leaves, jerking their arms up and out and shaking hands.

She felt a sharp kick and inhaled the smell of cedar, and the straight lines softened around her. She closed her eyes and the world outside the doors was gone, just like that.

The Only One

FOFI WOKE UP WITH a kink in her neck, as if it had been tilted at a weird angle all night. She'd had the dream again where she had to wear a futuristic helmet that looked like a big silver beehive, because she lived in a futuristic society and had to obey the law that said everyone had to wear helmets all the time. People also had to forage for food like wild animals, but at least they wouldn't be crippled by objects falling on their heads.

She and her fellow citizens were always staring into the sun. They wanted to blind themselves so they wouldn't have to see all the things that had gone wrong in the world. Then they would complain to each other that everything was so dark.

Fofi kept quiet, though. She was not one of those old ladies who moaned to everyone about her aches and pains.

THE HOSPITAL CALLED FOFI that afternoon.

"This is the Podiatry Clinic for Fofi Poulakis?"

"Yes?" Fofi muted the TV. She'd been watching a nature program about squirrels.

"Let me reconfirm the spelling for our records: P-o-u-l-a-k-i-s?"

"That's right." Fofi looked down at her feet and back at the screen. A black squirrel and a red squirrel were fighting over a pile of nuts. "Why are you calling here?"

"You're listed as the contact person for a patient Weaver."

"I am?" She squinted out her window at the grey clouds. "I don't understand. Doug died six months ago."

"Doug?" said the secretary. "No, our patient's name is Gloria Weaver."

"Gloria Weaver?" said Fofi. "I'm her contact person?"

"She's under some sedation here and requested that we contact you for a ride home."

"Sedation for her feet?" The squirrels were really going at it. Fofi was rooting for the red one.

"Sometimes they have to do a lot of digging around. It can be pretty painful."

"But how did she get there in the first place?"

"Look," said the secretary, "I have a bunch of other calls to make. Will you please come and pick her up?"

"Can you call someone else?"

"You're the only person we have down."

Fofi sighed. "All right."

"YOU'RE THE BEST, FOF," said Gloria in Fofi's car. "Next time I have my appointment, you say the word and I'll pick you up something nice at the gift shop."

"Next time?" Fofi squeezed the wheel. "What's at the gift shop?"

"Anything you want," said Gloria. "Are you kidding me? They got good stuff there."

Fofi eyed their reflections in the rearview mirror. They were both wearing sweaters and stretchy slacks, but Gloria's sweater had a nature scene on it — a forest, a river, howling wolves.

"I don't know," said Fofi. "They really overprice things at those places."

"Nothing's too good for you. For my contact person, the world."

Fofi braked hard at a stoplight. "How are you, Gloria?"

"It's the damn diabetes again. It's driving me crazy. They gave me this checklist for healthy feet. They say I've got bad blood flow." She lifted her right foot and wiggled it.

"I see you got your shoe on all right. That's good."

"Oh, but you should see the gauze around my big toe. It's like a mummy's toe. Ha!"

"Ha." Fofi stomped on the gas. "So I guess it's a good thing I was home, I guess."

"Even if you weren't, I would've tracked you down eventually. You're the only one they know to call."

"Right." Fofi turned into Gloria's driveway. "Here we are."

"Just be thankful you don't have diabetes, is all I'm saying. They gave me this list of things I'm supposed to do. Wash my feet, trim my toenails. Now, when Douglas was around, he would do those things for me. But now that he's gone, well —" Gloria wiped some lint off of Fofi's dashboard. "Be thankful you don't have diabetes and that your husband is still alive, is what I really mean to say."

"Gloria," said Fofi, "Albert left me for another woman."

The side of Gloria's mouth twitched. "That's right. Sorry, Fof. But you know what I'm saying — at least he's out there." She reached into her coat pocket. "Now, where did I put my keys?"

Fofi switched off her turn signal as Gloria searched around in both of her coat pockets, then went into her purse.

"I know I had them." Gloria rolled her eyes. "Oh, ow, the drugs are wearing off now, I think. I still feel a bit woozy upstairs, you know? But the pain is definitely coming back. Ow, ow. Where the heck are those keys?"

"I really should be getting back home, Gloria."

"Of course you should. You have things to do. Of course you want to go home. Fofi, I'm telling you again, you're the best. Okay, so they're not in my coat pockets and they're not in my purse. It's these damn drugs, they're making me so I can't think straight. They gave me a shot of — I don't know what they gave me a shot of, but it was pretty strong stuff." Gloria started to knock herself on the head. "My brain ... is ... not ... working ... properly."

"Gloria, you shouldn't do that to yourself," said Fofi. "Did you check your pants pockets?"

"Good thinking, Fof. This brain of mine, I'm telling you. Hold on, let me check." She patted herself down. "Nope. Not there either."

The two front windows of Gloria's bungalow stared back at Fofi. The driveway was a tongue lolling out of the closed garage door. "Do you maybe keep a spare key under a mat, or something?"

"Now that would've come in handy, wouldn't it? It would definitely come in handy right about now. But no, I don't have a spare key. With Douglas gone, I don't like thinking I've left the key to my house outside for some vagrant to find, and I don't trust my neighbours at this place. At our last place, yes. Those people were kings and queens compared to the people I'm living next to now. You don't even want to know the things these people get up to."

"Well," said Fofi.

"Well," said Gloria.

It started to rain.

"FOFI! HOW MANY CHANNELS you get on this TV?"

Fofi closed the fridge. "I'm not sure, Gloria."

Gloria was on Fofi's couch with her feet up, flipping through the channels. "They just keep going!"

Fofi walked into the TV room from her adjoining kitchen, and set a plate on the coffee table.

"Cheese!" Gloria leaned over and grabbed a handful. "And crackers!" She brought the snacks to her mouth with both hands and ate, showering herself with crumbs. "Now will you look at that? Look at me. Sheesh." She brushed the crumbs onto the couch. "I only have basic cable — I don't get all these specialty channels. But what good are they, really? Like here, this one's got a show about squirrels. Who wants to watch that?"

"I like that one." Fofi sat down on Albert's old La-Z-Boy, the only thing he'd left behind. "They were playing that earlier."

The two women stared at the screen.

"That black squirrel's stealing the red one's nuts, look at it go!" said Gloria. "Poor little red squirrel. Mother Nature, huh. What's she got to say for herself?" She changed the channel. COPS was on. The two of them sat and watched a couple of policemen arresting a prostitute.

"I love this show," said Gloria.

"I never watch it," said Fofi.

"Well, prepare to be blown away."

The cops bent the hooker over the hood of their squad car.

"Can they do that?" said Fofi.

"They can do whatever they want," said Gloria. "They're cops."

Next she found a reality show about wife swapping. In the show, two women switched families for a week. They had to live with a different husband and different children, and the whole time they missed their own families and they were always crying, and they didn't get along with the other people because it was a new household with unfamiliar ways of doing things.

Fofi interlaced her fingers while Gloria ate her food and wielded her remote control. "Did you call the locksmith?"

Gloria's mouth was full. She nodded at the TV. "Oh, I called him, all right."

Fofi leaned forward. "What did he say?"

"He said he'll come by tomorrow."

"Tomorrow?" Fofi looked out her window. It was getting dark. "He can't come by tonight?"

Gloria shook her head, and her perm wobbled. "The decline of customer service. That is what we're forced to deal with in this day and age."

"You could try someone else. We could go through the phone book."

"No, no. I always use this guy. He does good work. That, and he knew Douglas, he was friends with Douglas, so I trust him. You only want so many people having access to your key mold, you know? Once they've got your key mold, there's no telling —" Gloria hugged herself. "I don't want to think about it."

"You always use him? How many times have you needed a locksmith?"

"Well, when I had my car, you know. I locked myself out a few times there." Gloria sat up. "You want to order a pizza?"

THE PIZZA WAS COLD when it arrived.

"Tell him you're not paying for it!" Gloria shouted from the couch, already eating.

The delivery boy went pale. He had a hint of stubble on his cheeks, and long eyelashes that he fluttered at Fofi. "Lady, please — if I don't bring the money back, my boss'll take it out of my paycheque."

"Don't listen to him, Fof! He's lying!" Gloria yelled around a large slice.

"How much do I owe you?" Fofi asked him.

"Twenty."

"Here's twenty-three."

The delivery boy showed her his teeth in a wide grin, and closed his fist around the cash. "Thanks, lady."

"They'll tell you anything," Gloria said when Fofi closed the door. "You can't believe what they say, those pizza boys. They'll say anything to get a tip."

Fofi went to the kitchen for plates.

"Thanks for picking up the tab on that, Fof. I guess my wallet's with my keys, wherever that is. I should cancel my cards, like you said." Gloria gnawed on her crust. "Douglas and I used to get pizza once a month. What about you and Albert?"

"I cooked." Fofi handed Gloria a plate.

Gloria waved it away. "Thanks, but I'm done. I have to watch my intake, with the diabetes. I have to balance out my system. Do you have any orange juice? Or a chocolate bar? Anything sweet."

"Something sweet, really?" said Fofi. "Are you sure about that?"

"Sure I'm sure. I know the drill." Gloria's mouth was a straight line. "I've been living with this for a while now."

Fofi shrugged. "I'll see what I have."

"You should eat first, though. Don't worry about me. You sit and eat."

Fofi took Gloria's clean plate back to the kitchen. "No, that's fine. I'm sure I have something." She replaced the plate in the cupboard and looked in her fridge. "How's ginger ale?"

"Ginger ale. Now, why didn't I think of that? I love ginger ale. Douglas always kept a bottle of it around — it was our drink. I'd love some, Fof. You're the best, you know that?"

Fofi watched the back of Gloria's curly head while she poured her drink. She had opened a fresh bottle, and the ginger ale fizzed at her. She screwed the lid on tight and put it back in the fridge, then brought the full glass to Gloria.

Gloria took a long sip and closed her eyes. "Ahh. Now that brings back memories."

Fofi picked up a slice of pizza and put it on her plate. Before she took a bite, she contemplated the few shrivelled mushrooms and single limp pepperoni slice on top of the congealing cheese. It was the worst pizza she'd ever tasted.

"So I can sleep right here tonight." Gloria slapped the couch. "I don't mind. I'll probably need a blanket, though. And do you have some pyjamas I could borrow?"

GLORIA TOOK THE RED flannel nightgown Fofi had lent her into the bathroom to change.

Fofi put on her own pyjamas and stood outside the bathroom door. She heard the water running in the tub. "Do you need a towel?" she called.

"Thanks, but I already found a nice, fluffy one in your closet," Gloria called back. "I got a washcloth too. I might need some help in here, though."

"You want me to come in?"

"Don't worry — I'm decent!"

Fofi pushed the door open.

The lid was down on the toilet and Gloria was sitting on it, with her bare feet propped on the white rim of the bathtub. "I got thinking about that foot list the hospital gave me," she said. "I got thinking I should probably do what's on the list, so that way maybe I won't have to go back for another appointment for a while."

Fofi nodded. "Sounds like you've got the right idea."

"I need a little bit of help, though, if you don't mind."

"Sure. Do you need me to turn off the tap? Here —" Fofi turned off the tap.

"Thanks. But actually, Fof, I was going to ask if you could help me take off this bandage they put on." Gloria jerked forward with her arms outstretched, and leaned back with a grunt. "It's hard for me to reach."

"Oh." Fofi looked at Gloria wearing Fofi's nightgown, sitting on Fofi's toilet, propping her diabetic feet up on Fofi's tub. She looked at the bandaged toe, which had blood on it. "Okay."

"Thanks, Fof. You're the best." Gloria lifted her right foot and thrust it at Fofi.

Fofi bent over to unwrap the gauze but it was wound on tight, so she settled onto her knees.

"That's it, you've got it. You want to know the reason I put you down as my contact person?"

Fofi looked up. "Why?"

"Because you came over after Douglas passed away. You brought that casserole and you sat with me at the table while I ate it. That meant a lot to me, Fof."

"It wasn't such a big thing, Gloria."

"No, no. It was, Fof. It was a huge thing. Friendship is important in this life. I feel sorry for people who don't have friends. They're like animals, barely existing."

Fofi tugged at the gauze. As she unravelled it, the brownish stain on the outer layers became redder. When she was finished, she dropped the bandage into the trashcan and eased herself back up. She washed her hands in the sink, scrubbing hard. "I guess I'll leave you to it, then." She backed toward the door.

Gloria examined her toe and winced. "Do you see that? That's what they have to do when your nail's ingrown. They have to dig it out. The doctor told me the nail penetrates the skin like a knife. That's why it's so painful." She coiled a permed curl around her finger. "Douglas used to kiss them. He would kiss my toes. Can you believe that? Did my husband ever kiss your toes?"

"What?"

Gloria looked at her in a cool, appraising way, and laughed. "Oops, oh boy, did you hear that? I meant your husband. Did Albert ever kiss your toes?"

"No, never." Fofi felt the doorknob pressing into her lower back.

"Douglas wasn't into toes in a weird fetish way, or anything. He just loved me so much." Gloria folded her hands in her lap. "Did Albert ever love you so much, Fof?"

"No." Fofi shook her head. "He never did."

Gloria smiled at her. "What it says on the list is, I need to wash my feet regularly. The doctor said there was absolutely no cheating on that." She pursed her lips. "You know something, could you do me a favour? The list is in my coat pocket — could you go and get it for me?"

"Sure." Fofi hurried out of the bathroom and closed the door, and walked down the hall past her bedroom, kitchen, TV room, to the closet by the front door. She unzipped one of Gloria's pockets and reached inside, and felt the piece of paper there. Then she felt something else.

Fofi pulled out the list, and Gloria's wallet and keys, and held them in her hand. She stared at the keys and the wallet for a moment, then put them back in the pocket and zipped it closed. She walked up the hall to the bathroom and opened the door.

"Did you find it?" said Gloria.

Fofi took a breath and gave her the paper. "Right where you said it would be."

"You really are the best, Fof." Gloria unfolded the page and held it up. "So what it says is: *Wash your feet daily and dry them carefully, especially between the toes. Keep toenails trimmed and smooth. Check for warning signs: redness, swelling, warmth, pain, slow healing, dry cracks, bleeding corns or calluses, tenderness, loss of sensation.*" She handed the list back to Fofi. "What I'm saying to you, Fof, is I need your help with that."

Fofi watched steam rise from the bath water as Gloria lowered her feet in.

Gloria handed her the soap and the washcloth. "Only because I can't do it by myself."

Fofi looked at Gloria's raw and swollen big toe, with ragged creases of new scab on either side of the thick, yellow nail. The soap was slippery in her palm and the washcloth was soft.

Then she nodded, slowly, and eased herself down onto her knees again.

Community

ON THE EARLY MORNING subway ride home from the cast party, I'm just like all the other guys here. We're leaving behind wild times that went all night. Our eyes are half-closed, and some of us are asleep.

In the seats across from me, three big teenage boys are passing a red Bic lighter back and forth.

The guy on the left says, "Fuck, I am so hungover."

The middle one says, "Fuck, I think I'm still drunk."

I nod, because I know what they mean.

The guy on the right rubs the lighter, unlit, against his jeans. He flicks the lighter on and touches the flame to the same spot.

"I swear to you," the middle one says, "this is supposed to work."

THE PLAY RECEIVED EXCELLENT reviews in both the local papers, so the lead actor, whose name is Sean, is now pretty much a star in his own right. One writer said he "moved like a god," which in most cases would be an exaggeration, but Sean was actually playing God, so if he hadn't been moving like one, then something would've been seriously wrong with his performance. All of this critical acclaim would have excused him if he had given me any sort of high-and-mighty attitude at the cast party, but he didn't. He was completely kind in every way.

Sean was sitting on the director's couch, and I was standing across the room, eating chips. The chips were good; they tasted like hot dogs. There's a new trend to make chips taste like food, even though they already are food. As if the chips would be nothing without the food-tasting powder sprinkled on.

The party was a potluck because in community theatre, everybody has something special to contribute. I had brought the chips. Nedra, the lead actress, had brought homemade date squares. I do not like date squares, have never liked them in the history of my life, but Nedra was smiling at me from beside Sean on the couch, so I took one to be polite. I put the heavy, sticky lump on my snack plate along with the chips and grapes that I was keen on eating. When I'd finished the chips and grapes, I took a nibble of a tiny corner of the square's oatmeal topping. I was trying to avoid the inner mushed-up-dates part, which made me think of the tar sands, which are basically dinosaur toilets, if you want to get scientific.

Nedra said to me, "What do you think, Gerald? It's my mother's recipe."

I said, "Good!" and put my plate down when she looked away. I wanted to kick myself. Why did I even take it in the first place, knowing I wouldn't enjoy it? I thought about my own mother, who never made a date square in her life, and I loved her for that. Her specialty was pie. She even told me once, "Gerald, we are all made of various slices of pie, and some of us have more lemon meringue or coconut cream in them than others. Then you have the mincemeat people."

Nedra fell into the mincemeat category. She was wearing a sparkly green gown that looked like a wizard's robe, and I pictured her casting an evil spell on me as punishment for rejecting her potluck contribution.

Sean put his arm around her, and said in a loud voice, "Gerald is allergic to date squares, Nedra. You don't want to kill the poor guy, do you?"

I was confused for a second because I wasn't allergic, but then Sean winked at me. "Yes." I nodded. "You're right, Sean. Thanks for reminding me."

"I got your back," he said, and squeezed Nedra's knee.

I felt a bit sorry for her then, since she had no idea what was going on.

When Nedra did her monologue, which was mostly a lot of crying and wailing, "Why, God, why?" after Sean's character slipped on a giant oil slick and fell off the end of the Earth into The Hell Of Our Own Making, the audience applauded, and nearly all of them stood up. She got a standing ovation during the play! But there was one lady who remained seated. I could see the crowd by peeking out from behind the curtain, and this woman was the only one still in her chair, frowning at the stage. All around her, dozens of hands were flying and whacking each other, but she didn't move a muscle.

My first thought was maybe she was religious and was offended by the play's content, but then I remembered seeing her laugh along with her fellow audience members when Sean tripped over an elephant that had been slaughtered by ivory poachers (the idea behind his character was to show God's clumsiness, or in other words, His humanity), so it probably wasn't the content that offended her. My next thought was that this lady must have a lot of guts to be so firm in her likes and dislikes, to sit there alone and go against what everyone else was doing.

I am pretty much an enigma, as far as what others know about me. People don't pry, and I'm fine with that. Not too many people were talking to me at the cast party, or I should say, no one was, at least for the first few hours. At rehearsals, they would say, "Hey, Gerald, can you move that chair over here?" or "Hey, Gerald, that backdrop needs something. More poisonous smog clouds, maybe?" And I was only too happy to oblige.

But Sean was different, right from the start. He saw my potential. At the first all-hands meeting when the cast and crew sat in a circle and introduced ourselves, I said my name is Gerald, and Sean said, "Did you say Harold?" I said, "No, with a G." He said, "I like Gerald better than Harold." Then after the meeting, Sean said he was going to Slam Dunk's for wings and a pitcher, and did anybody want to go with him and run lines? Nedra batted her eyelashes at him and said she'd love to but she had plans with her daughter, and the other cast and crew members all had plans with their families too, but I said, "I'll go with you, Sean." And Sean said, "Gerald, my man."

We had an ant problem on set for a while because of Nedra. She didn't properly dispose of her prop sandwich, which was actually a real ham sandwich that she only took two bites of in the scene. She was supposed to put the sandwich in a plastic bag after and take the plastic bag home, but she just left the sandwich sitting on the stage all night. The next day: ants everywhere.

At home, I was not attending to the various things that needed doing in my apartment, upkeep things, because I was so worn out from keeping up the set — or, as the director would say, the psychic space in the hive-mind of the audience — in a pristine condition. Which of course I didn't mind in the least, and the gratitude I could feel emanating from those around me made it all worth it. I would find messes at home, spills and crumbs and nests of stray hairs, that I would never have tolerated on set.

At the party, the actors were all on one side of the director's living room and the set techs were on the other, which is how it went most of the time at the theatre during rehearsals. The actors, with the exception of Sean, of course, who is cut from a different cloth, something rugged like burlap or denim, are the type of people who look down upon non-actors. During rehearsals we would all take our breaks at the same time, but there was that definite separation between cast and crew. Still, we all played our parts in crafting a successful production, as the director kept telling us. And she hosted the cast party for all of us because we all played our roles so well, both onstage and off.

Yesterday morning, before the party, I was excited. I woke up and thought to myself, *I am going to have a pleasant morning, afternoon, and night.* I had breakfast, washed the dishes that had been piling up in my sink since the play started, then went for a stroll and picked up my Jägermeister. I was excited about the Jägermeister because there were people in the cast who I wanted to get closer to. I was going to get drunk and they were going to get drunk, and the party would get crazy and then we'd see what happened.

The set pieces I built included, but were not limited to: an African savannah, the Louisiana coastline with a bunch of gunked-up birds and small mammals, and The Hell Of Our Own Making. It only took me five days to build Africa and three days to build Louisiana. Hell took a bit longer because of the conceptual component. One of the reviews said the set was "very realistic looking." I have a woodworking background, which is a definite plus in set creation.

If you got up really close to my set pieces, you would probably see little cracks, holes, blank spots, imperfections. But the idea is to step back and observe the whole picture. I created an illusion, and the overall effect is what needs to be judged. Don't overlook the branches for the leaves, or whatever it is they say.

At the cast party, it was problematic to go to the bathroom because the director's kitten was in there. The director told us she had to keep the cat away from everybody because there was something wrong with her. She was too violent. So every time I went in there, I had to defend myself against this little ball of fur and claws and teeth that kept catapulting itself at me.

On set, there was a prop telephone with an old-fashioned curly cord that I liked to pick up every so often. I would hold it to my ear for a joke and go, "Hello? Hello? Who's there? Wrong number!" And then hang it up, forcefully. It was a riot, and a few people, including Sean, laughed almost every time. Otherwise, I mostly kept to myself.

When we took our lunch breaks, I'd eat my cold-cut-combo sub in the back, making sure not to leave any crumbs. There were ant traps everywhere, which the actors kept kicking accidentally, and they would skid like little red-and-black hockey pucks across the stage. I brought cold-cut combos every time because they have three types of meat and I needed the protein blast for the long days.

People came to me when they needed things fixed, and I liked that. On the first day when the director brought the cast and crew together, everybody was extra nice to each other — "Looking forward to working with you!" and slaps on the back all around. But then the cast stopped talking to the crew and generally only talked to other cast members, and the crew didn't talk to anybody.

But let's be reasonable here. We were all family, the cast and the crew. And the set techs, like me, were on exactly the same level as everyone else, which is what the director told us from the beginning. When one of our cast family members was in need, we attended to that need.

When Sean and I went to Slam Dunk's, there were big screens everywhere with different games playing on them, all these superior athletes throwing themselves at each other and throwing things at each other. Sean ordered us wings and beer that we ate and drank, and then he wiped his hands carefully with a wet-nap and pulled out his script. He said, "I only have the one copy, so you'll probably have to skootch up closer so you can read the other lines." I said, "Sure, I can skootch." He read his lines, and I read everybody else's, and the TV crowds cheered all around us.

At the party, the director's TV was tuned to an animal bloopers show, and we all watched a confused moose head-butting a tire swing that somebody had hung up in the woods. Everybody hooted along with the laugh track when the swing kept flying back to bonk the moose when he wasn't looking, and he'd jump. Then he'd head-butt the tire again because he was freaked out and probably pissed off too, and it would swing away and swing back and bonk him again. He'd jump and turn around and lower his antlers, and take another run at it. I felt kind of bad for laughing at him, but it was funny.

I pride myself on being creative and also efficient. I loved it when people referred to me as their "go-to guy." Once there was a prop emergency, and the director came to me. She needed a bread box, pronto, for Nedra to put the loaf of bread in after she made her sandwich. There was another layer to it as well, since it was supposed to represent the Breadbox of Heaven, where the baby angels were born, and the bread was their pillow.

The director told me that we didn't have anything left in the budget, so I went to Value Village, but the closest thing they had was a butter dish, so I went to Goodwill, where they had a cake plate but no bread boxes. "Who uses bread boxes anymore?" said one of the Goodwill employees when I asked for help. I told him, "It's for a play." He said, "Ahh," and looked at me like I was someone important. He brought me a silicone muffin pan, which was both the wrong thing and too modern. The play was about a fortune-teller in the 1950s who predicts a bunch of future environmental disasters and ultimately the complete destruction of the planet. So we were going for realism in the props.

After all that, I went to my apartment as a last resort and dug up some old scrap metal I had lying around in my workshop, and I built a bread box from scratch. I took it back to the gang, and Sean called me, and I quote, "a hero."

For my "day job," as the actors like to call it, I am an unemployed carpenter. So you can imagine how much I enjoyed working on this play. It gave purpose to my days. There was something beautiful about constructing an artificial universe for people to move around in and pretend to be other people in. Even though that artificial universe was damaged beyond repair by humankind's shortsighted greed in the future, AKA the present (like I said — layers). It was all make-believe, but it meant something. Because eventually, people bought tickets and sat in the seats and watched the drama unfold, and were spellbound. Their experience was enriched by the actors' hand gestures and by the made-up words invented by some writer who may still be alive or may be dead, but regardless his words continue to live on in the immortal pages of the script. It was inspiring to be surrounded by art all day, which is what life in the theatre is all about.

It was a pretty amazing feeling to watch the actors and actresses acting out fake emotions, which, let's face it, are basically partly real under the surface. They couldn't possibly be totally fake when they said the things they said, or they would have to be robots. For instance, Sean is a very talented individual in the realm of show business, but at the cast party when he said, "Gerald, I like you, buddy," I had to believe him, at least a little bit.

When I woke up this morning on the director's living-room floor, it took me a few minutes to orient myself to the unfamiliar location. Then I saw my empty Jägermeister bottle, and Nedra's pan of date squares, looking like the particle-board model I built of the desiccated Fertile Crescent, and it all came flooding back.

The house was very dark and quiet. The living room was empty, except for me. I walked down the hall to the bathroom, and stood at the door listening to the kitten's claws scratching on the other side. I couldn't believe this little animal's energy and determination. Over and over — *scritch, scritch, scritch*. It didn't even meow.

I looked at the other two closed doors. Then I opened one, slowly, and peeked inside. The director was sleeping in her bed with her husband, Bill. They had their arms around each other. I closed their door and opened the other one, and stepped into that room.

A thin beam of light was coming in through the blinds, like a spotlight right on Sean's face. A reviewer would probably write that he slept like a god. And then the lump beside him. Nedra. I stood on the soft carpet. My neck was stiff from sleeping on the couch, but I didn't want to rub it.

Sean's face was peaceful. He was so at ease in front of an audience. I wondered where he got his confidence from. At Slam Dunk's, he asked the waitress if they actually used brand-name hot sauce or if they just filled up brand-name bottles with the generic stuff, and she said she didn't know. He made a gun with his hand and pointed it at her and said, "Don't make me interrogate you, now." And she blushed and giggled like she was having a fit. He was so dynamic, I wanted to squeeze all the acting juice out of him, make it run out of his ears and nose and mouth, everywhere. He had that kind of effect on people.

ON THE SUBWAY, THE boy on the left lights his pants on fire. The small flame jumps across his jeans like a live thing, and he watches it for a few seconds before blowing on it and slapping it out. "Holy shit, did you see that?" he yells at his friends. "I did it!"

I smile, and I remember how the director told me at one point in the evening that they had my phone number, so they can call me if they need me. If and when my services are required again by the theatrical community, they have my contact information. She said I'm on a list.

I imagine my name and number, copied out in careful handwriting on a crisp, white sheet of paper in the director's Rolodex or whatever, or maybe even taped or tacked up somewhere, and that mental picture makes me feel better about the world. And although, as the play dramatically illustrated, it's ugly and unfair and it stinks, it's our world, which is a really nice thing to think about.

The Plant Lady

THINGS ARE GOING WELL for Mandy these days, so she can't help worrying that something is going to go wrong soon. She thinks this on her way to work on Monday morning, and the thought deflates her lingering happiness about the weekend, when she and Jim had walked through a field together.

Their walk had the movie quality that everyone strives for, with the wide-open blue sky and the sun in their eyes and the green, green grass that seemed to go on forever, until they reached the end of it and had to turn around and walk back.

MANDY WORKS IN THE office at a stencil factory, but a lot of people are under the impression that she works at a pencil factory because A) she doesn't like her job very much so she tends to mumble when she is asked about it, and B) she never elaborates.

"Where do you work?" people will ask her.

"Stencil factory," Mandy will mumble.

"Ooh, pencils! What's that like?"

"Let's talk about something else," Mandy will say.

THE PLANT LADY COMES by Mandy's desk at five-thirty.

This is the first time Mandy has ever been in the office after five — this morning her boss asked her to stay and work late on an outline for a new project and she thought, *Like hell*, and smiled and told him of course she would, and then she had to call Jim and let him know he'd have to wait for dinner (he said he'd get takeout) — so she has not met the plant lady before. But she has heard stories.

For instance, when she told her co-worker Brenda earlier that day that she had to work late, Brenda said, "Uh-oh. Better watch out for the plant lady."

"Who's the plant lady?" Mandy had said. (She is remembering this exchange as she observes, out of the corner of her eye, a middle-aged woman with shaggy, yellowish-white hair dribbling water over the potted palm in the far corner of her cubicle.)

"Trust me, watch out. She'll talk your ear off if you let her, and you'll never get rid of her."

"Brenda, that doesn't sound like something you'd say," Mandy had said, because Brenda is the type of woman who wears collared blouses with embroidered, non-functional pockets, and keeps a dish of individually wrapped mint toffees on her desk.

And Brenda had squinted her already small eyes at Mandy as she made her final pronouncement before ambling off down the hall: "Keep your distance, Mandy, if you know what's good for you."

Which Mandy generally does know, except right at this

moment she is sitting no more than two feet away from the very plant lady she has been cautioned about, who says to her in a voice filled with quiet menace, "I always wondered who sat here."

"Hi there!" Mandy says, too loudly. "You must be the person who keeps this office so nice and green! I'm Mandy." As soon as those last two words are out of her mouth, she remembers the warning she got from Piadora, the office skank, who had cruised past Mandy's desk after talking with Brenda and said, "Don't ever tell her your name, or you'll regret it."

Well, what does she know? thinks Mandy, though she is secretly jealous that Piadora wears tube tops every day and never has to fidget with them.

The plant lady unhooks a spray bottle from one of her belt loops, hooks her heavy eyebrows over her heavy-lidded eyes. "I'm Cathy. Think you can remember that, Mandy?"

Hmm, Mandy thinks, and says, "I think that's do-able."

"You think that's do-able, who?"

Mandy blinks at her once, twice, three times — "Cathy! I think that's do-able, Cathy."

"Very good," says Cathy the plant lady. "You would be appalled by the number of people around here who don't take the trouble to remember my name. I'm just the plant lady to them. I'm just a service provider. They go home, they come back the next day and surprise! Their plants have magically watered themselves. Personally, I think it's funny that most people never take the time to think about how that happened."

"I guess I'm not most people."

"I can see that, Mandy." The plant lady looks her over. "I can see that."

Mandy gives her mouse a perfunctory shove before her screen-saver comes on.

"Working late?"

"Unfortunately." She rolls her eyes at her monitor.

"Don't want it to turn into a trend, right?"

Mandy nods, shakes her head. "Ha, ha, yes, no."

"Husband at home?"

Mandy isn't sure if she means, "Do you have a husband at home?" or "Is your husband at home or is he somewhere you don't know about?" So she gives a non-committal half-nod to her new acquaintance, who is now spritzing water over the fern on Mandy's desk, and says, "I like that fern, how small it is."

"It's a dwarf."

"Ohh, don't say that —" Mandy reaches around the fern, pretending to cover its ears. "You'll hurt its feelings!"

The plant lady stares at her until Mandy returns her hands to her lap. "Plants don't have feelings, Mandy."

"No, ha, ha. I know that, I was only —"

"A lot of offices are doing everything dwarf these days. Personally, I think that's going too far." The plant lady gives the little fern one more spritz from her water bottle.

Mandy feels a few of the cool droplets land on her face. "You've got a nice, quiet job, looks like."

"Oh, you get into conversations with people, doing this kind of thing. The other week I'm over at the head office and the VP is working late, and she tells me her mother just died."

"That's awful."

"It gets worse. Then she opens up and talks to me for an hour and a half. I walk into her office, start in on the Chinese evergreen, and she goes and tells me her life story. An hour and a half this woman talks to me for. Some people, all you have to do is come along when they need someone to talk to, and you're it."

"Huh." Mandy sneaks a peek at the clock on her screen when the plant lady isn't looking.

"Now, though, after all that, she won't talk to me anymore. Guess she regrets opening up so much, being so candid. But that's fine, whatever, that's her choice." The plant lady gazes over Mandy's shoulder, tightens her grip on her watering can. "She won't even look at me."

"Well." Mandy coughs again, discreetly. Smiles in an apologetic way. "I should probably get back to work."

"Oh, of course." The plant lady takes a giant step backward. "I didn't realize I was disturbing you."

"No, no, you're not disturbing me, no way." Mandy's stomach plummets. "I have to get home soon, that's all."

"To your husband."

"Well, he's there, yes."

The plant lady stares at her for a good fifteen seconds, then says, "Welcome to the working-late club, Mandy." She executes a grim salute with her spray bottle before heading off down the hall.

"Ha, thanks." Mandy watches her go, and feels a flicker of foreboding with the realization that she has already forgotten the plant lady's name.

MANDY AND JIM WON an expensive lawnmower in a hospital lottery about a week ago, and now Jim has decided that they're going to try to get store credit for it at the Home Depot, since they sell that same sort of lawnmower and have a good return policy.

"Imagine all the great Home Depot crap we could get for what that mower's worth!" he says. "And it's failsafe." He's standing in the middle of the living room, flicking the ticket against the underside of his chin. "Either they take it back or they don't."

"Or we go to jail."

"We will not go to jail. If anything, Home Depot gives us a slap on the wrist. Or they call in the cops to give us a slap on the wrist. A slap on the wrist is nothing."

She takes off her office shoes and lies on the couch. "I can't be a part of this. It's bad karma to screw a hospital."

"But it's not the hospital we're screwing. That's the best part! We'll be screwing an American big-box-store chain."

All this talk of screwing makes Mandy think maybe they should have sex. Maybe both of them should become inflamed by all this talk of screwing, and rush at each other, rip and tear at clothing, claw at bare skin. But she is still lying on the couch and he is still standing there with the winning ticket in his hand, saying again, "Either they take it back or they don't."

"Remember that walk we took?" she says. "On the weekend? How blue the sky was and how green the grass was?"

"What made you think of that?" says Jim. "We're talking about Home Depot here."

Mandy sighs. "I just don't think it's the honest thing to do."

"Of course it's not. The honest thing would be to take the mower. Except, and here's the problem —" He touches a finger to his nose and then points that same finger at her. "We don't have a lawn."

"But that's our problem."

Jim throws up his hands, and the ticket goes flying. It floats through the air, as graceful as any airborne hospital-lottery ticket has ever been or could ever hope to be. They both watch it fall and at the last second, Jim plucks it up, saving it, and Mandy applauds in spite of herself.

IN THE FIELD, THE sun had been so bright that Mandy had needed to shield her eyes. Jim had reached for her other hand and said, "This is the first perfect day of the year."

Mandy looked at him. "Tell me something."

"Like what?"

"Something you're thinking."

Jim squinted into the distance. "I think Gary's lonely."

Gary is one of Jim's sports-bar friends. Every time Mandy has seen him, he's had a few spots of wing sauce on his face. Wings and wing condiments seem to be the only things that Gary ever eats.

"Oh." The field went on and on, green stretching as far as Mandy could see.

"Yeah. The guy's been single forever."

Mandy was holding hands with Jim on the wrong side. Her right hand was in his left hand, and his wedding ring was digging into her knuckles. She liked it better when her wedding ring was digging into him.

"The thing about Gary is, he needs to put himself out there more. He's either at the sports bar with me or he's at home watching a game. I told him, 'Gary, you need to get out there.' And you know what he said to me?"

She scissored her fingers to loosen his grip a little. "What did he say?"

"He said, 'Jimmy, I've been out there, and there's nothing.'"

THE THING IS, SOMETIMES a voice whispers in Mandy's ear, *You're going to be alone. You are going to be alone.* And sometimes when she cuts through the office parking lot on her way to the bus stop, she thinks that cars are circling her like sharks. But of course this imaginary voice doesn't know what it's talking about (she has Jim, after all — he married her), and the cars are just waiting for her to move out of their way before they pull into a parking space or roll out of the lot.

"THEN RON WAVES OVER the cabana boy, and says, 'Make that piña colada a double, on the double!'" Mandy's friend Sheila slaps herself on the thigh. "Ha! Oh, those men of ours, eh Mandy?"

"Sheila, that's too much." Mandy shakes her head and puts a loonie in the machine on the bar for another serving of Hot Nuts.

Sheila got back last week from another trip with her husband — a resort in Cuba this time, all-inclusive. She is tanned and happy. "You want to hear the punchline? Ron wouldn't even drink his. Said it was too strong. So I had to drink both of them, ha!"

Mandy takes a big slug of her rum and Coke, which, she is thinking, is as close to Cuba as she's going to get. "You know if it was me, Sheil, I wouldn't be drinking piña coladas because I can't stand pineapple. Everyone always says, 'Ooh, pineapple!' But it's one of those flavours I never developed a taste for."

"Look at us, eh?" Sheila leans forward on her stool and slaps Mandy on the knee. "Two broads who've been abroad!"

The farthest Mandy has ever travelled was to Florida in the 1980s with her parents, but she doesn't remind her bronzed friend about this, she just nods and sips her drink.

"So what's new with you?" says Sheila.

"Jim fixed our drip on the weekend with his new Home Depot tools. In the bathroom."

"God, Ron couldn't fix a drip to save his life."

They are sitting at the bar next to two young guys who are trying to pick up two young girls. The guys are firing off jokes and the girls are giggling at them.

"We're closing in on our fifth wedding anniversary, can you believe that? Five years." Sheila whistles. "We'll probably go to Rome or Spain for this one. Somewhere with a history. What's five years anyway, tinfoil? Ha! Who knows."

"We're getting near our third. That'll be seven years I've known him. How long have I known you, Sheil?"

"Too long," her friend says, and they both grin and clink their glasses together.

The joking and giggling of the guys and girls beside them has grown louder, so Sheila has to raise her voice over the din — "Can we get another round?" she yells to the bartender. "We're talking about old times here."

JIM IS IN THE bathroom the next morning, turning the sink faucet on and off. Mandy watches him from the kitchen table.

"There are no ifs, ands, or buts about this tap," he says. "It's either on or it's off. There's no in-between anymore."

"It's nice the way it doesn't drip."

Jim turns and beams at her. "Isn't it?"

"Your cereal's getting soggy."

He walks over and sits down. "So how's Sheila?"

"Oh, you know Sheila. Saving the world one piña colada at a time."

"Then you've got nothing to be jealous about," Jim says, chewing. "You hate pineapple."

"What do you mean, jealous?" Mandy puts down her spoon. "I'm not jealous."

"Where did she and Ron fly in from this time? Spain?"

"Cuba. They haven't been to Spain yet."

"Yet, right? 'Yet' is the operative word." Jim leans back in his chair, slides his empty bowl away. "What a life. Drinking on a beach all day. Then again, they're childless."

Mandy picks up her spoon again. "We don't have kids yet either, Jim."

"Aha, but there's that 'yet' again. There is no yet for Ron and Sheila, right? So they spend their savings on all these getaways."

"They don't want to have babies." Mandy pokes at one of the no-name oat rings bobbing in her milk. "It's something they've agreed on."

"Then everything works out, doesn't it?"

Mandy pushes her chair away from the table. "I should get ready for work."

ON THE BUS, MANDY begins to compose a list of the things she has to do for Jim's sister Gretta's baby shower, which Mandy has been asked to organize.

Things to Bring to the Shower, she writes. *Food*, she writes next, and decides that will have to be a subhead. *Decorations*, she writes a few spaces down, and underlines both words.

Mandy doesn't really know any of Gretta's friends, but she has been asked to organize her baby shower because, as Gretta put it, "It's what sister-in-laws do." Which Mandy can't really argue with, but at the same time she can't figure out why Gretta picked her, because Gretta doesn't like Mandy very much.

Gretta invited Mandy to her sewing circle once, and Mandy brought one of Jim's shirts that was missing a button. "I'll just sit here and sew on this button," she'd said.

And Gretta had said, "That's a mockery. It's a mockery of Collette's afghan, Regina's toaster cozy, and my embroidered Welcome To Our Home poem."

Mandy had looked at the three women with their dangling threads and poised needles, and thought, *This isn't even a circle, it's a square. It was a triangle before I got here.*

The bus slows as it passes a school, and three boys lingering by the bike racks look directly into Mandy's window. She waves at them, and the tallest one yells, "Slut!"

When Jim is in the mood to be seduced, Mandy will hear him singing from some part of the house, "Oh Mandy, well you came and you came and it's raining. But you'll sit here someday, oh Mandy." She's pretty sure that's not how the real song goes, but that's the way he sings it. It's their code. She'll follow the sound of his voice to wherever he is, and when she finds him he'll either be naked or on his way to being naked.

When Mandy is in the mood, she'll look at Jim and wait to see how long it takes him to look back at her. If it's longer than the time it takes her to count to ten in her head, her mood tends to go away.

Lately, Mandy has been noticing that the times when she is in the mood have been fewer, and Jim hasn't been singing so much lately either. But still, they're both happy, aren't they?

Gretta is an OB/GYN nurse and Mandy wonders if maybe she should speak with her about the situation. She's not sure if she and Gretta have that kind of relationship, but she has even less faith in Dr. Proctor, her family physician, who is breezy about the things Mandy feels are important. *Is it even a medical thing, though?* she thinks. *Is it even worth mentioning?*

"THESE LEAVES ARE DRIVING me crazy," Mandy says to Brenda at the end of the work day, which is not really the end for Mandy because her boss has asked her to stay late again. She waves a hand at the tendrils dangling from the overgrown plant on the top shelf of her desk. "Look at them. They're a mess. They've been distracting me all day."

"You better make sure the plant lady doesn't hear you talking like that," says Brenda.

"What's she going to do?" says Mandy. "Water me?"

At that moment, there is an unmistakable *snip, snip, snip* from the other side of Mandy's cubicle.

Brenda's little eyes get big and she backs away. "I'll see you tomorrow."

"Brenda —" she says, but her co-worker is already halfway down the hall.

The snipping continues, and Mandy hears the clearing of a throat. The tangle of unruly leaves begins to shake, and an unseen force pulls them up until they are no longer cluttering her workspace. Then the plant lady comes around the corner with a large pair of garden shears and an armload of green cuttings.

"Heyyy," says Mandy. "It's you!"

"That's right." The plant lady tightens her grip around the

fronds and stems. "It's me."

"Ha, and there I was saying that these leaves are all over the place, and you're one step ahead of me. With the scissors."

"You didn't say they were all over the place. You said they were driving you crazy. That's what I heard."

"Right. Ha. Yes. I guess that is what I said. But, you know, six of one and all that. And thank you, I mean, for trimming the leaves. I was starting to feel like I was in that movie with that killer plant — what's the line?"

The plant lady sets the garden shears down on Mandy's desk with a clack.

"'Feed me, Seymour!'" says Mandy. "That's it. You know the one I mean? What was it? *Little Shop of Horrors*. With that big plant, that killer plant with the teeth."

"You knockin' my work, Mandy?"

"Ha, ha, no!" Mandy rocks forward in her chair. "I was only drawing a comparison, the way the leaves were hanging all over the place —"

"By saying those things, you're saying that I haven't been doing my job properly. A workplace plant should be decorative yet unobtrusive. You're saying the plant was intrusive." The plant lady lets her arms drop to her sides, and the bushel of cuttings she's been cradling falls to the ground like waxy green teardrops. "Just because you may be unsatisfied in some arena of your life doesn't give you a license to dump all over mine."

"What? I'm not unsatisfied."

"Say what you mean and mean what you say." The plant lady crosses her arms, tilts her head. "I bet you don't even remember my name, do you, Mandy?"

Mandy presses herself against the unyielding foam of her backrest. "Um."

The plant lady stoops to pick up the cuttings, laughing to herself, and when she straightens back up she says, "I'm just giving you a hard time, Mandy." She plucks the garden shears from Mandy's desk. "It's Cathy."

"Of course, yes. Cathy." But as soon as she says the name it's gone, because at the same time she's thinking, *Am I unsatisfied?*

MANDY MEETS SHEILA AT the bar after work, and the first thing she says is, "What's my problem, Sheila? I mean, really, why am I so uptight?"

"You have your strengths and your weaknesses, like everyone else. Nobody's perfect." Sheila downs her booze and wiggles two fingers at the bartender.

Mandy thinks, *That wiggle is the difference between me and my best friend.* She says, "But look at you," and waves a hand at Sheila, who is wearing a skirt while Mandy is wearing capris.

"I don't know." Sheila shrugs. "I don't let things get under my skin, I guess."

Mandy takes stock of the cold glass in her hand, the padded comfort of the stool beneath her. They come to this bar because it is not one of those bars that have mirrors everywhere. "I think I'm stressed out."

"Stress is for suckers."

"That's easy for you to say. You and your vacations." Mandy gazes down the bar and sees a woman roughly her age who is wearing the same length of capris as her. The pants make the woman's ankles look like tree trunks, even though the woman herself is not particularly large. Mandy crosses her legs at the calf and tucks them as far under her bar stool as she can manage.

"What you need," says Sheila, "is a night on the town with Jim." Mandy opens her mouth, but Sheila holds up a hand. "And not one of your monthly outings to Mother Tuckers with a coupon either. I'm talking a hotel here. I am talking about hotel sex."

Mandy's mouth is now a straight-across firm line. "We are not the type of couple who does that sort of thing, Sheila. Jim would not go for something like that, I can tell you right now."

"All I'm saying is, don't knock it until you try it. I'm serious here, Mandy. This is serious business." Sheila leans forward on her stool. "Do you think Ron and I sit across from each other sipping piña coladas all day at those resorts? Sure, there's a bit of that going on. But I am telling you there is flinging down and jumping on top and pounding against the wall, Mandy. There is reaching into his swim trunks in the deep end of the pool bar and moving aside the crotch of my tankini bottoms and there is gripping the ladder for dear life and then —"

"Hold on!" says Mandy. "Sheila, hold on one minute. That's just too much."

"It's never too much," says Sheila. "Not when you're on vacation, it's not."

"THE TAP IS DRIPPING again," Jim says with a sad face when Mandy gets home. "I can't figure it out."

"What would you think about a hotel sometime?" she asks him.

"What about it?"

"Us. Together. In a hotel room. Renting one, I mean."

"But we have a house," says Jim.

"That's the part I can't quite figure out either," says Mandy.

"I DON'T KNOW, MANDY," Jim says once they've checked into the Travelodge that weekend and are sitting together on the edge of their double bed. "I'm not sure if this kind of thing is for us."

"Don't knock it until you try it, Jim." Mandy slides into a horizontal position on the floral-patterned bedspread and puckers her lips at him. "What are you thinking of, right now?"

"I was thinking of turning on the TV," he says, in a kind of apologetic way.

"Fine." She lies on the bed while he fiddles with the remote control and finds *Unsolved Mysteries*. "Not this," she says. "Anything but this."

"But I like to solve the mysteries."

"I know you do. But we're not here to solve mysteries. We're here ..." Mandy thinks for a bit, "... to be mysterious."

"What does that mean?"

She sighs. "We're too familiar with each other. Let's pretend to be strangers."

"But I like being familiar."

"I do too. I'm only talking one night here, Jim."

The host of *Unsolved Mysteries* glares at them and asks, "Will we ever know what happened to this ill-fated couple?" And from the other side of the wall behind the TV, a woman's voice says, "Ahhh!" and a man's voice says, "Ohh."

Mandy and Jim look at each other with wide eyes, and Jim hits the mute button.

The sounds get louder, building to a see-sawing crescendo.

Then quiet murmurs, some laughter.

Jim stares at the wall and whispers, "Do you think they're better at it than we are?"

Mandy puts a hand on his leg. "They just make more noise than we do."

"All right." He puts the remote down. "Let's give this pretending thing a go."

"Really?" She grins and sits up. "Okay. You don't know me and I don't know you. I'll go into the bathroom, and when I come out, we'll both assume our characters."

"Who do you want me to be?"

"Whoever you want."

Mandy goes into the bathroom and shuts the door. Everything is white — towels, tiles, porcelain — except for the little potted plant on the white counter. She rubs one of the leaves and realizes it's plastic, which makes sense because there aren't any windows in the bathroom, so how could a real plant grow?

There's a knock on the door, and she opens it.

"Can't we just be Mandy and Jim?" says Jim. He's in his pyjamas. "It feels weird otherwise."

"Okay, Jim." She gives him a small smile.

"Hey, free soaps!" He walks in and picks up one of the miniature bars on the counter, next to the artificial plant. The way he holds it, gently between his thumb and forefinger, makes Mandy want to run.

"IT COULD BE ANY number of things," Dr. Proctor tells Mandy the next day. "The way you feel about your body, the way you feel about your husband."

"But I love my husband."

"I'm sure you do." Dr. Proctor picks a bit of fluff off of his golf shirt. "However, we can't rule anything out."

"This is a very embarrassing thing for me to discuss," she says.

"I'm sure it is." Dr. Proctor inspects the fluff.

Breezy, she thinks. She says, "Is there something I can take? Or something Jim can take?"

"Oh, there are things you can take, of course there are." He settles back into his big leather chair. "But I am not a prescription factory here. I don't like to be pulling out my pad and my pen until I'm absolutely certain that's the right thing to do."

"Of course. So what else would you advise?"

"Have you tried ..." Dr. Proctor waggles his hands in the air, "... spicing things up a bit?"

"Um." She looks away from his hands to the framed degrees on the wall behind him, the bright red seals on the bright white paper.

"For one thing, I would recommend taking a vacation. Couples often find a change of scenery very helpful."

Mandy laces her fingers together. "We can't really afford a vacation right now."

"Sometimes even a night in a local hotel can have an invigorating effect."

"We tried a hotel."

Dr. Proctor slides an inch or two forward. "And?"

Mandy hangs her head. "We stole a bunch of little soaps and then we both got a good night's sleep."

"Well." Dr. Proctor smiles, and pats both of his knees before standing up. "That's something, isn't it?"

BREEZY, MANDY THINKS AGAIN on her way home.

And besides, she's never been able to get past the rhyme.

MANDY MEETS SHEILA FOR drinks after work, and Sheila tells her that she has started a blog. "I've joined the online community, Mandy. I'm out there!"

"Huh." Mandy nods. "What kinds of things are you writing about?"

"Blogging about."

"Right. Blogging about."

"Oh, you know, my life and all that. My username is Angel Hair, isn't that awesome?"

Mandy shifts her position on her stool. "Like the pasta?"

"No, not like the pasta. Well, I guess, yes ... maybe." Sheila frowns. "Damnit, I didn't think of that."

Mandy takes a big slug of her Zombie — Monday is $3 Zombie Night. "Anyway," she says. "You have a blog."

"Yes, I have a blog." Sheila claps her hands a few times, applauding herself. "Everybody talks to each other in short form. I'm using words like 'sitch' now, isn't that great?"

"What's a 'sitch'?"

"It's short for situation. Isn't that hilarious?"

"I don't know," says Mandy. "What about the cyber-stalkers?"

"Oh, it's all harmless. I'm never going to meet any of these people."

"I saw a special on Internet predators." Mandy nods upwards, where the original *Night of the Living Dead* is playing on the TV mounted over the bar. "There's a lot of them."

"Jesus, Mandy. The predators are after the twelve-year-olds."

"Does Ron have a blog too?"

"He doesn't actually know about it," Sheila says, a bit quickly. "It's a thing I'm doing for me."

"Oh," says Mandy, and they sit for a while in silence, watching the black-and-white carnage overhead.

"JIM," MANDY SAYS TO Jim the next morning, "what's Gretta's schedule like these days?"

"She's working fewer shifts. But I'm sure the baby preparation is taking up a lot of her time."

"Like ... buying things for the baby?"

"There's that." He nods. "But also the other things. The preparation. Darren was telling me."

When Mandy told Jim she was Gretta's baby-shower organizer, Jim said, "Don't go getting any ideas now!" Which, coming from Jim, meant he really did want Mandy to get ideas.

"But what other things?" she says.

"Mandy, if you don't know ..."

Mandy is about to say, *But I don't know*, but what comes out instead is, "I was thinking it might be nice to have lunch with her."

"Her shower's tomorrow. You'll see her then."

"I know. But it would be nice to have some private time."

"Really?" Jim glances up from his cereal. "What for?"

"She's your sister," she says. "Why wouldn't I want private time?"

THERE IS A MELON at the baby shower that has been carved into the shape of a bassinette. Mandy stares at it, admiring the slick, orange contours.

"Mandy?" Gretta calls.

Mandy looks over at her sister-in-law, who is reclining on a La-Z-Boy adorned with plastic rattles and cellophane storks. Around her neck are close to twenty soothers on pink and blue strings, their rubber tips bobbing on the curved shelf of her bulging midsection. Her belly is the biggest belly in the room.

"Yes, Gretta?"

"The streamers on that side of the room have gone limp."

Mandy peers across the living room, which belongs to Crystal, Gretta's best friend from college. Gretta had insisted on using Crystal's house as the shower venue, because she "feels more comfortable there."

"Can you tape up the corners for me, Mandy?"

"Sure, Gretta." Mandy puts down her paper plate of pita triangles with ham. "Do you know where the tape is?"

"I think Bo Peep had it last."

"Bo Peep" is Gretta's nickname for Crystal that no one but her is allowed to use.

"Leave it to me." Mandy stands up from her metal folding chair, and the thin cushion on top makes an exhausted sound.

Gretta's mother Kiki, who is also Mandy's mother-in-law, is making a chain out of the various ribbons and bows she and Gretta's mother-in-law have peeled off the shower gifts. The two older women are perched on either side of the mother-to-be, and they watch Mandy as she passes.

"Grandchildren are a blessing, aren't they, Darlene?" Kiki says to Gretta's mother-in-law.

"A blessing from God," says Darlene.

"Amen to that!" Gretta says, and she reaches up to adjust her

"I'm Expecting!" tiara with one hand and fondles her collection of trophy pacifiers with the other.

Kiki untangles a bright, frilly knot with a yank. "They say the longer you wait, the drier your tubes get."

The other women snicker behind their melon-slice smiles.

"That's right!" Crystal shouts over. "Your tubes turn into beef jerky if you wait too long!"

Aside from hostessing, which from what Mandy has observed entails owning the house and not much else, Crystal has not been a big help with the shower. She is now, as she has been since two o'clock when things got underway, sitting under the strung-up paper baby-bootie cut-outs with a Styrofoam glass of lemonade-and-Cointreau punch.

Mandy stands in front of Crystal's balloon-festooned seat and does a quick scan to ascertain the location of the tape, but doesn't see it anywhere. "Crystal, do you have the tape? Gretta says you had it last."

Crystal leers at her over her punch. "What're you gonna give me for it?" she says, her breath coming at Mandy like a wall of citrus.

"Bo Peep!" Gretta hollers from across the room. "Give my sister-in-law the tape, you whore!"

"Ha, ha!" yells Crystal. "I love you, Gretta!"

"I love you too, you skeeze!"

"We're just giving you a hard time, Mandy," says Crystal. "You can't take things so seriously, you know?" She fishes the tape roll out of the folds of her skort, which she'd made a show of flapping up and down when the party started, saying, "You get the best of both worlds with this thing — it's shorts, but everybody thinks it's a skirt so you freak them out when you do this!"

Mandy fits her hand through the mouth of the roll. Then she walks over to the streamers Gretta has taken issue with and peels off two strips of tape for the corners.

WHEN MANDY GETS HOME that night, Jim is not in the living room and he's not in the kitchen. Then she hears something.

"Oh Mandy, well you came and you came and it's raining ..."

Mandy's shoulders are throbbing from taking down all the decorations under Gretta and Crystal's supervision. Gretta had wanted to keep everything pristine and un-ripped for the next time she has a shower, because she and Darren are going to start trying again right after she gives birth, and Crystal was concerned about tape marks on her walls. "Watch the walls!" she'd yelled every time Mandy went to un-stick a banner or a diaper wreath.

"... but you'll sit here somedayyy, oh Mandy."

She finds Jim in his briefs, sitting cross-legged on their bed and grinning at her. He's holding something she can't see. "How was the shower?"

"We played lots of baby games."

"Oh yeah? Like what?"

She stands with her sore arms at her sides. "Everybody got a soother on a string and if you crossed your legs or said the word 'baby' you lost your soother."

"Sounds like fun." Jim reaches a hand out to her. The other one is still balled up between his legs. "I hope you didn't get any ideas!"

"I'm pretty tired, Jim. I have to go to bed now."

"Come on in." He pats the duvet.

"I mean I have to go to sleep," she says, and then, "I'm not really in the mood."

"Oh. Okay. I'm going to have another go at the faucet, then. The dripping is driving me crazy." And before he gets up and walks past her out of the bedroom, he gives her a sad kind of half-smile and opens his hand, and she sees the little hotel soap he's been hiding.

MANDY STAYS LATE AT work again the following week.

At five-thirty, when everyone else has gone home, she heads to the staff kitchenette to give her mug a rinse, and freezes in the doorway.

The plant lady is in there, standing at the sink and filling her various cans and bottles. She's facing away from Mandy, and Mandy backs up, slowly. Her first thought is, *She's here*. Her second thought is, *My God, I've forgotten her name again*.

She returns to her desk with her dirty mug and holds her hands over her keyboard, then places them in her lap. *Cheryl*, she thinks. *No — not Cheryl. Charlene? Christine? Cassandra?* The names cycle through her brain faster and faster, but none of them sticks.

She listens to the water running in the kitchenette, waits for the silence that will signify the tap has been turned off. And there it is, the absence of sound. Until she hears the clanking and sloshing behind her. But she doesn't turn around or give any sign of acknowledgement. She doesn't have to, she reasons, because the plant lady hasn't officially announced her arrival — she hasn't actually spoken to Mandy yet.

"Mandy!"

"Haaa," Mandy breathes, and swivels on her chair to see the plant lady, with her watering cans and her spray bottles and her down-turned mouth. "Hi!"

"Thought you'd never turn around."

"Ha," Mandy says, because nothing else comes to mind. "I was immersed, I guess."

The plant lady cocks her head, squints at the rows of data on Mandy's computer screen. "Immersed. That's a new one."

"How are you?"

"No complaints." The plant lady looks left and right with a fake-wild expression. "This isn't the Complaints Department, is it?" She laughs a loud and bitter laugh. "Is there one around here? Because I can't find it."

"Ha."

The plant lady's smile unfolds itself one corner at a time. "Burning the midnight oil again, are we, Mandy?"

Mandy's eyes dart to the time display on her screen. "It's only five-forty."

The plant lady's arms bristle with long spouts. "You've got a point, Mandy. And me just starting. We live parallel lives, you and I. But you know something that bothers me a little bit, Mandy? We're both people, right? We both have lives that we're living. And we both have names. Now, I know your name, but you don't know mine. How is that supposed to make me feel? Not very good, is how."

"Cindy!"

The plant lady shakes her head slowly back and forth, a metronome of disapproval. "No, Mandy. You've got it all wrong."

Mandy's phone rings, and she grabs for it. "Hello?"

"Mandy, guess what?" It's Jim. "Gary's in love!"

"Hold on a sec," she says, giving the plant lady a "What can you do?" shrug and wobbling the handset at her.

"Guess I'd better get watering then," the plant lady says tonelessly, and moves away.

"Thank God, Jim," Mandy whispers into the receiver. "Thank God."

"You're telling me," he says. "The guy's been single forever."

"No, I meant because I was ... never mind." She glances over her shoulder at the empty office behind her. *Where is she?* she thinks. "So what happened?" she says to Jim.

"Gary called me up and spilled his guts over this girl he met. I think it's the real deal, Mandy — I think this is it for the guy."

"What, out of the blue like that?"

"Out of the blue, ha! That's a good one — you know, because of the blue cheese dip he likes? He'll get a kick out of that, Honey. I'll pass it on."

Mandy closes her eyes then, and she's back in that field with Jim. The sun is pounding down and the sky is so blue it hurts to look at it, and the green-green grass is so long it's curling up around their ankles.

"He went to a service providers' convention on the weekend. She had a booth. He says they totally hit it off. First he pretended like he was interested in her booth. Or maybe he really was interested, I can't remember. I'm so happy for the guy! She's an editor. Works with words. 'Watch out,' I told him. I said to him, 'Your grammar sucks, so you better watch what you say to this one.'"

Mandy cradles the receiver. "If she's right for him, he should be able to say anything he likes."

Then the plant lady comes back around the corner.

"I have to go," Mandy whispers into the phone, and hangs it up very gently before focusing on her monitor.

The plant lady stands next to Mandy and crosses her arms, which is a difficult manoeuvre with the two watering cans she's holding. "You like it here, Mandy?"

Mandy's shoulders tighten and she hits the space bar a few times. "It's all right."

"Yeah? I love it. You know, when I started working here, nobody ever worked late. I had the place to myself every night, just me and the plants." The plant lady leans forward. Up close, her shaggy hair looks overgrown. "And you want to know something else, Mandy? Plants don't judge. All they ever do is sit there and let you take care of them."

Mandy's phone rings again. "I should get that."

"Yes, of course. Don't let me get in the way of all the important work you have to do."

"Ohhh, that's — you're not —"

"I've got work of my own to do here." The plant lady starts to drip from her right elbow, where a watering can has tilted out of her grasp. "Damnit! Can't I do anything right?"

"Sorry, I'd better —" Mandy picks up the phone. "Hello?"

"Mandy," says Sheila, "I've got some crazy news."

"Tell me." Mandy's screen has gone black with her screen-saver. Before the pinpoints of light begin star-bursting out at her, she sees the plant lady's reflection turn and walk away, all slumped shoulders and bulging handles.

"So there's this guy," says Sheila, "on the Internet. He's been posting all these comments on my blog."

Mandy frowns, fidgeting against her backrest. "And?"

Sheila giggles. "And I think I like him."

"Sheila. You're married, remember?"

"But that's the best part! This thing I'm telling you about — it's only virtual."

A loud crash on the other side of the office makes Mandy jump.

"Anyway, Ron wouldn't understand. The other day I was all excited about this quiz I put up, called 'What's Your Funky Inner Hair Colour?' That's the great thing about blogs. If you can't think of anything to write, you can go to these sites and pop in quizzes for people to do. And I tried to get Ron to give me his answers but he said — get this — 'That's dumb.'"

"It is dumb. How can a hair colour be inner?" She looks left and right, but doesn't see the plant lady anywhere. Something about the office is different, though.

"They mean what colour your hair is inside. They're talking about the hair colour of your soul."

Bang! "Oh my God." Mandy spins around, but the cubicle walls and desks and chairs all appear normal under the bleak fluorescent light.

"I know, it's priceless."

Mandy peers up at the tiny perforations in the ceiling tiles, and over at the farthest dark corners of the room. Something is missing, but she can't put her finger on what. "Sheila," she says. "Ron loves you."

A pause. "Oh, I know that."

Then Mandy realizes that the colours are wrong, because

except for her potted palm and dwarf fern and the formerly unruly plant on her top shelf, there's no green anywhere.

BEFORE SHE GOES HOME, Mandy walks into the staff washroom and opens one of the stall doors. And takes a step back, because the toilet is filled with leaves. They're sticking out of the bowl at all angles, almost as if they're growing there.

Mandy moves to the next stall, and sees the same thing. One by one, she opens the stall doors. All of the toilets have been stuffed with green — torn leaves, broken stems, ripped vines. She decides she doesn't really have to pee that badly, and heads for the exit. But she feels something different than the regular floor beneath her shoes, and looks down. More leaves, strewn across the tile. And even though there shouldn't be a breeze in the staff washroom, something is making the loose length of paper towel flutter on the roller.

Mandy exhales and realizes that the air is coming from her.

"SO," GRETTA SAYS THE next day, slicing up her tuna wrap, "Jim says you wanted to have lunch."

"I did." Mandy looks down at her soup. "I do."

They are sitting at one of the long tables in Gretta's hospital cafeteria. Mandy had asked if they could meet somewhere else, but Gretta is "more at ease in this environment." They are surrounded by chattering hospital staff, many of whom Gretta seems to be acquainted with.

"Tina, you slob!" she yells now at a petite blonde in pink scrubs, who is nibbling on a small salad at the next table. "Use a napkin, why don't you?!"

Tina chuckles and shakes her head. "You're a riot, Gretta!"

Mandy dips her plastic spoon into her Styrofoam bowl of chicken gumbo, disturbing the yellow globs of fat on the surface.

Gretta is one of those pregnant women who doesn't gain any girth beyond the midsection. Mandy tells her that now, and Gretta pulls at the elastic on her yellow scrub pants and says, "Yeah, people say I don't look pregnant from the back. That is the best compliment you can give a pregnant woman — say she doesn't look pregnant from behind and she'll be your best friend."

"You really don't," Mandy says, but Gretta isn't listening.

"Alonzo, you slug! Put down that knife and fork and eat your pizza like a man!"

The handsome, broad-shouldered doctor a few tables over gives Gretta a warm smile and hails her with his stethoscope.

"So," says Mandy, "how's the baby preparation going?"

"Is that why you wanted to have lunch?" says Gretta. "To talk about babies?"

Mandy crosses and uncrosses her legs under the table, which is an uncomfortable height. "Sort of."

"Because as you can see —" Gretta pats her swollen stomach. "— I don't really have much to tell you yet."

"Right, no, I know. Hey, but this is nice. Spending some time together."

Gretta raises a neatly tweezed eyebrow at her. "We saw each other at the shower."

"Of course, sure. But this way we can —"

"Dwayne!" Gretta stands up to holler some abuse at a nearby orderly, and her giant belly rises in front of Mandy like the sun.

If We Dig Precious Things from the Land, We Will Invite Disaster

IT SAYS IN THE florist's horoscope today that he needs to let go of pettiness, and that he is destined for greatness but that his path to greatness will be littered with the bodies of the cherished people, places, and things in his life.

The florist rips some leaves off the unruly blue hydrangea that has been pissing him off all day. It's too hot, it has been too hot all summer, and the hydrangea mocks him with its fluffy coolness.

He looks up when a woman walks into the store, the chimes tinkling over her big head. The woman's head is large. She walks right up to the florist and orders a mound of carnations. This is the word she uses — a *mound*.

The florist pictures how he would make a mound of carnations. He would chop off their heads and peel off their leaves and snap their stems in half and fling all the pieces to the floor. Then he would tell this woman to sit on it. Her mound.

The woman asks him, "How old are you? Shouldn't you be in

school or something?" Bats her eyelashes. Her eyelashes are long, sticky, vampire things.

The florist says, "I'm older than I look." He is still pulling apart the hydrangea.

The woman says, "My, you're strong, aren't you?"

He says, "It's only a plant."

"About those carnations ..."

"Yes, how many?"

"You tell me."

It's only a matter of time before he reaches for the scissors, or the letter opener he uses for the bills, or the label maker he uses for price tags and the other petty things in his life. Label makers are deadly because of how easily they define things.

The woman smiles at him. "I'm thinking pink," she says. "It's for breast cancer." She tells him she is organizing a run for the cure, and that her name is Nancy.

THE ALLERGIST DRAWS TWO lines of dots on both of the florist's forearms with a blue Bic pen.

The florist thinks, *A Bic? He doesn't have a special allergist's pen?*

The allergist dabs the blue dots with different tinctures, then uses a tiny needle to prick those places. He moves fast with the needle, jabbing up to the top and back down to the bottom like it's a race. When he finishes, he tells the florist, "Now hold out your arms, like this."

The florist says, "I don't feel anything. Am I supposed to feel something?"

The allergist says, "Wait."

The florist waits in the waiting room for an hour with his

palms turned upward so the tinctures won't run off. It's difficult to turn the pages of a magazine with his arms in this position, so he just sits there and stares down the ficus tree in the corner. *It must be fake*, he thinks. *They wouldn't keep a real plant in here, with us.*

A fellow patient smiles at him in a collegial way and holds out her own blue-dotted arms. "It itches, right?"

"No," he says. "Is it supposed to itch?"

"If you're allergic. You're really not itchy? Jesus, I want to crawl out of my skin."

The florist starts to panic a little, and wills himself to get itchy. He figures it's only a matter of time.

At the end of the hour, the allergist asks the florist to come back into his office. He inspects the florist's arms, wipes them clean with a swab, and says, "I usually see some reaction, but you had no reaction at all."

"I think I felt something at one point," says the florist. "I'm pretty sure. Where was the flower area?"

The allergist gestures at the smooth, pale skin on the florist's left forearm. "No redness, no bumps. You showed no reaction to flowers, dust, dogs, cats, shellfish, nuts — none of them. You are allergic to nothing."

"I'm a florist."

"That's good news for you, then."

The allergist's desk is cluttered with medical reference books and inhalers and bottles of sinus rinse and a clear plastic case containing the pinned bodies of (according to their labels) a common housefly, a horse fly, a bumblebee, a hornet. One of the allergist's walls is almost entirely covered by an anatomical diagram of a wasp. It's so big that the florist imagines he can hear buzzing. The venom sac is shaped like a teardrop.

"People are allergic to everything these days," says the allergist. "Some of them can't even leave their house. They're allergic to grass, tree pollen, insect stings, cold, sunlight. Sunlight! Like vampires. And we're doing it to ourselves. Polluting our air, drinking and eating out of plastic all day. The rainforests. There is an ancient prophecy that states, 'If we dig precious things from the land, we will ignite it faster.' I heard that somewhere once, and it stuck with me. Think about it." The allergist smiles at the florist and picks up a small microphone. He presses a button on a voice recorder and dictates, "Patient has no allergies, full stop."

THE NEXT DAY, THE florist prepares Nancy's pink carnation mound.

He doesn't chop off the heads or peel off the leaves or snap the stems in half and fling all the pieces to the floor. Instead, he arranges the flowers into a bulbous hillock culminating in a pointy tip.

When Nancy comes in to pick up the bouquet, she holds it out in front of her and then hugs it to her chest, stroking the ruffled petals. "I want to keep it for myself," she says. "But I guess I have to give it to the winner."

"All you have to do is win, then."

"Oh, I don't participate. I'm just the organizer." She tells him she started organizing the runs for the cure after her husband left her, which happened after she hired a de-cluttering expert to de-clutter their house. "He never liked things the way they were," she says, "so I thought this would be a good birthday present."

The expert came in and told them to get rid of a lot of things. She said they should look at a thing and ask themselves if they really needed it. She pointed an accusing finger at their big, heavy filing cabinet, and Nancy's husband pointed at Nancy and said, "That's hers."

"What do you have in here?" the expert asked her.

Nancy shrugged. "Old files."

"Be specific. Open it and look inside."

Nancy pulled out a creaky drawer. "Bank slips. Warranties. Postcards. Letters. Concert tickets. The instructions for the coffee maker. My vaccination record from when I was a teenager. Breast self-exam booklets and booklets on how to identify suspicious moles. I have cancer in my family, that's why I kept those."

"Burn it all."

Nancy's husband really got into it. He shredded and purged and tossed and scoured while she sewed buttons back onto their jackets and mended the holes in their socks. "Things are falling apart," she said to him, and he told her to stop being dramatic and then he donated all of his old clothes to charity. He rolled up all of their spare change and took it to the bank and bought a new wardrobe, even though their original plan was to go for a nice dinner with the extra money.

One day they were standing in the middle of their living room, which was piled with boxes of things they'd realized they didn't need anymore, and Nancy's husband turned to her and said, "I don't need you anymore."

She smiles at the florist. "And then I got cancer."

The florist touches the buttons on his cash register. "I went to see an allergist because I hoped I was allergic to flowers, but I'm not. I look around in here and all I want to do is sneeze. I don't like flowers, but I'm good at arranging them. People love my bouquets. They say, 'How could someone so young make something so beautiful?' I tell them I'm not so young, but they keep coming back for more."

"My husband never brought me flowers. He said they would just die anyway."

"They're already dead," says the florist. He traces the contours of Nancy's big head with his eyes. It's mostly because of her hair, he realizes. She has a massive hairdo.

She catches him staring and says, "It's a big wig."

"Oh, I wasn't —"

"Ha, get it? Bigwig. I get a kick out of saying that. I got it when all my hair fell out from the chemo. I figured I might as well have fun with the wig, since none of the rest of it was fun. My hair's growing back now, but it's still really short so I'm still wearing the wig." She rocks the pink bouquet in her arms. "We were going to have a baby."

ON THE BUS RIDE to work the next day, the florist sits behind a man and his small son.

The father says to the son, who is maybe five, "I don't want you to have to grow up so fast that you don't have a childhood. I don't want you to feel too much pressure. But you have to remember that you are *numero uno*. You are my first-born son, and with that comes a great responsibility. You have to set a good example for your little brothers when I'm not around, and you have to be nice to your mommy because your mommy is not like your daddy. Your daddy gets mad and yells at you because he wants you to be safe and do the right thing, but your mommy gets mad and yells at you because she has anger inside of her."

The bus passes a red and yellow sign, and the son's breathing becomes rapid. "I want a hamburger."

The father shakes his head. "The food at McDonald's is garbage. You only like their burgers because they give you a toy with them. That's how they get the kids." He pats his son on the head. The son's hair is curly, and the father's hand bounces up and down. "Just remember that you have a very special purpose, and you will know what it is when you are ready."

"McDonald's," the son says.

The father says, "We'll go to the park later."

A siren howls, and the son bangs on his window. "Fire truck, Daddy!"

The florist pulls the dinger for his stop. He steps off the bus and walks the block to his flower shop, which is in flames.

While he stands there with his keys dangling, watching the billowing smoke, Nancy the breast-cancer woman comes up behind him and whispers in his ear, "Now I want you to do something for me."

NANCY TURNS OFF HER bedroom light and says, "Take off your shirt."

The florist takes off his shirt. He doesn't feel uncomfortable doing this, because it's hot in Nancy's apartment, and dark, with just the dim red glow of her digital clock to illuminate his bare chest.

She asks him, "Why did you become a florist if you don't like flowers?"

"I just fell into it. You know how people can fall into things."

Across the room, a device similar to a walkie-talkie hisses and crackles.

Nancy sees the florist looking over. "I bought that baby monitor when I still thought I was going to have a baby, to test it out. I kept it because it picks up my neighbours having sex."

The florist nods, listening for moans in the static.

"I have this theory that babies are plotting to take over the world," she says. "There's this one baby, and over on the next block there's another baby, and another and another, and they all send telepathic messages to each other over their baby monitors. It's creepy, I know."

The florist has pancake nipples. They lie flat and brown and smooth, and he is ashamed that they haven't puckered into arrowheads because of being here.

Nancy slaps her knees and stands up. She walks over to her window, which holds a badly fitting air conditioner. "Okay, so I have tried to figure out, to the best of my ability, how to secure this air conditioning unit in my window. But it's very precarious and I'm running out of ideas. I tried to shim it with wood, mostly because I love the word *shim*. I ripped pages out of the newspaper with the intention of balling them up to stuff in the crevices, but the articles were all interesting or horrifying so I read them instead. I squeezed glue around the edges of the unit and pushed it farther back so the glued parts would stick to the window ledge. Then I closed my eyes and wished for the glue to set, and while I was at it, I wished for all of my dreams to come true, which include working somewhere I'd like to work and meeting someone I'd like to know, and maybe someday moving somewhere I'd like to be, and then staying there for a while, but not too long because then I'd be stagnating, and that is the exact opposite of what I'm trying to do here, the way I'm trying to live my life."

The florist wants to applaud, but instead he stands up and goes to the window and puts her air conditioner in place. Afterwards, when it's cooler, he puts his shirt back on.

NANCY CALLS THE FLORIST at home the next day and tells him that she had her faults too. She was jealous and insecure. It got in the way of the good things in her marriage.

The florist is happy to listen because he doesn't have to go to work, because there is no work to go to. He isn't a florist anymore. He is an ex-florist with an insurance cheque in the mail.

Nancy's husband had a female friend at his office and he talked about her all the time. The three of them went for dinner one night so the two women could meet each other.

Nancy smiled through the meal and made polite conversation, but the whole time she was comparing herself to the female friend. Like how Nancy was wearing a nice enough sweater and jeans, and the female friend was wearing a similar sweater and jeans, yet she had somehow put the whole outfit together in an effortless way that looked incredibly polished and pretty, and how Nancy had never been able to pull off a look like that. She wanted to ask the female friend where she shopped, but she was afraid to. The stores would either be out of her price range, or they would be the same places Nancy shopped, which would mean that Nancy really didn't have a clue about fashion at all.

After dinner, the three of them went to a bookstore, and Nancy immediately lost sight of her husband. The store was huge and the shelves were tall and there was a main floor and an upstairs and a basement. He could have been anywhere, running his fingers along book spines with his female friend.

She didn't want to look for him, to see if he was with her. She didn't want to crane her neck or stand on her tiptoes to peer over shelves because then it would look like she didn't trust him. Because she did. It was more the nagging feeling that he would rather be with anyone but her. The books held millions of other possible lives that he could be leading, without her.

Then he appeared at the end of her row, grinning and alone, and asked if she'd found anything she liked.

NANCY AND THE FLORIST have sex. She removes her wig for him, and without it, her short-haired head is very small. Beneath the camisole that she said she preferred to keep on, her breasts are two perfect globes. He thinks how wonderful it is that cosmetic surgery has come so far these days. He also worries about puncturing them.

Afterwards, Nancy tells him that if there's one thing she's gotten good at, it's goodbyes. She has become an expert at them. She just goes to that place where she doesn't need the person in her life anymore, and she says goodbye, or maybe she'll only think it, and then it will be easy to stop returning that person's phone calls or emails. She'll almost forget that person ever played a part in her life, though of course not entirely. She files them away and they became clutter, and she knows how to deal with clutter now.

"My whole life I have been either underestimated or overestimated because I look younger than I am," says the florist.

"In the summer, I hear kids playing all day in that big park across the street," she says. "In the winter, I hear the squeals of kids going down the hill on their sleds all day."

A woman's magazine is lying open on her bedside table, and the florist reads to himself, *Some of the hottest things to do to a man are things he will not expect, and will not see coming.*

Nancy gets out of bed and comes back with an empty beige sack that she lays on the florist's belly. She smoothes her hand over it and him and says, "This was my colostomy bag."

"Oh," he says, "I guess I figured breasts because of the fundraising."

"People don't want to run for colon cancer," she tells him. "They think it's gross."

NANCY AND THE FLORIST walk to the florist's house later that night because Nancy says she wants a change of scenery. On their way past the park, a parade of pre-teen girls appears and encircles them like a cell membrane with ponytails and lip gloss.

The tallest girl extends her slender arm to show them something tiny crawling on it, and says, "Want to pet my mouse?"

The other girls giggle in an uproarious way, and the smallest girl of the group says, "She means our mouse."

"We have two!" shouts a round-faced girl, and her hand shoots forward with another mouse perched on it.

"We're going to take turns looking after them," says the tall girl.

"We love them!" says the round-faced girl, who has a big spray of Queen Anne's lace tucked behind one ear. The florist thinks, *She thinks that's a flower, but it's actually a weed.*

The tall girl bends her head to kiss her mouse, and her long hair covers it like a lush curtain. "We're too young to buy pets from the pet store on our own, so we asked a mechanic in the auto shop to buy them for us."

"He thought we were sexy!" shrieks the smallest girl, and they all laugh in a high-pitched, wheezing way.

"We have named our mice Mrs. Lady Horatio Duncecap and Mr. Lord and Lady Pickle Pie," says the tall girl.

"You can't call him 'Lord and Lady,' that's stupid." The round-faced girl tugs the Queen Anne's lace free and offers it to her mouse to sniff. "It should just be 'Lord'."

"Which one do you think is cuter?" the tall one asks the florist, and both girls hold out their squirming friends for his inspection. "We're having a competition."

He looks for a while and then says, "They're both equally cute."

"Liar!" the smallest girl yells, hopping up and down.

"Really, they're both very nice."

"But mine is the cutest."

"No way! Mine is the cutest!"

The florist hears a sound, and realizes that Nancy has started to cry.

"What's wrong with her?" says the tall girl.

The round-faced girl drop-kicks her weed onto the sidewalk. "She's just jealous."

THE FLORIST SLEEPS IN the next morning. When he wakes up to sunlight flooding his bedroom, he reaches out for Nancy but she's not there.

He looks around for a note or anything she might have left

behind. The room is tidier than he remembers it ever being, even though they messed everything up when they arrived last night — an overturned wastebasket now righted and emptied, her clothes gone from the floor and his clothes folded and placed on the chair by his bed, the previously rumpled sheets tucked in neatly around him.

The florist takes a deep breath and stretches out under the millions of dust motes spotlit overhead. A wasp buzzes outside his window screen, trying to find a way in.

He feels a tickle at the back of his throat, and he coughs, then sneezes. His eyes start to water and his nose starts to run. His ankle itches, and he reaches down to scratch it. He lets out a long sigh while he digs red furrows into his skin with his fingernails, which still have a stubborn layer of dirt under them.

He lies there and waits while the itch travels up his legs and spreads to his groin, his torso, his chest, his neck, to the crown of his head and out along his arms to his fingertips, until all of him is on fire.

Ear, Nose, and Throat

JODY'S POLYP IS RUINING her life.

Her boyfriend Teddy doesn't think it's a big deal, but Teddy doesn't think anything is a big deal. Before they slept together for the first time, Jody told him that she had never had an orgasm, and Teddy said, "That's cool."

"It's not, actually," she said, but they slept together anyway.

Jody and Teddy are lying in bed, listening to the roofers. The pounding and swearing has been going on for days now. It wakes them up in the morning.

"Yesterday I heard them comparing prison experiences," Teddy whispers. "They've all been in prison."

A shadow appears against their blinds, and Jody says, "Shh."

Bang! "So my buddy's wife is all into that organic shit, right? I was over one time and I ask her does she have any coffee, and she says no, but do I want a cup of hot water. I said, 'Are you fucking serious?' She says it's good for your insides, it's the best thing you can do for yourself. So she gave me the hot water, and I fucking drank it."

Bang! Bang! "I'll give her something to warm up her insides with!"

Teddy puts his mouth against Jody's ear. "There are criminals on our roof."

"Shh!" She blows her nose quietly and pulls the covers up to her neck. On the other side of the window, the dark shapes wield their big tools.

TEDDY IS THROWING A surprise 43rd anniversary party for his parents in a few months. "It's their 43rd," he says. "Why shouldn't they have a party? They made it this far."

They're making the save-the-date calls now, which Teddy asked Jody to do because she has the better phone voice.

Most of the people she calls have no idea who she is, and she has to explain to Teddy's parents' friends and relatives and neighbours and former co-workers that she is Teddy's girlfriend. Yes, Teddy has a girlfriend. Eight years. Oh, no, ha, no ring yet. We live together, yes. We're saving up money to buy a condo. Oh, sure, a wedding before then. The date is May 5th. Make sure you park out of sight of the house. Another street is perfect. No gifts, please. If you'd really like to bring something, you could bring a bottle of wine, that would be nice. No, I haven't been crying, I'm just stuffed up. I'm sure he will, yes, one of these days. Great, we'll see you there. No, I don't have a cold. Yes, I'm looking forward to meeting you, as well. No, ha ha, no kids. It's not allergies. I have a nasal polyp. No, it's not cancer. It's a fleshy swelling on my sinus lining. May 5th, that's right. It was nice talking with you too.

Jody carries a potted plant around the apartment while she makes the calls.

All of their plants are dying, but Jody is convinced that if she keeps moving them around until they find a place they like, everything will be okay.

When Teddy's mother comes to visit, she caresses the drooping yellow leaves and winks at Jody and says, "When you have my grandchildren, will you kill them too?"

Jody forces a laugh and shakes her head, but sometimes she waits an extra day or two to water the plants, just to make a point. She has heard that over-watering is worse than under-watering, anyway.

When Jody hangs up on the last guest, Teddy says, "We should do tapas for the party, like a whole bunch of miniature finger foods."

"Hmm. That could get expensive, couldn't it?"

"I'm just talking a shitload of President's Choice appetizers here. Nothing fancy. But it should be stuff you heat up in the oven. People like the hot stuff."

"It might get pretty warm in May with the oven on."

"Stop being so negative," he says. "It's a party."

Teddy is studying hospitality at George Brown, and whenever he cooks at home, he wants Jody to call him "Chef."

"How about I call you that in bed?" she'll say to him with wiggling eyebrows, and he'll say, "Why would you do that?"

IN LINE AT THE grocery store, Jody blows her nose and says to Teddy, "I hate this. I'm stuffed up all the time, or else my nose is constantly running."

Teddy says, "Then why don't you catch it?"

They load their items onto the conveyor belt — radicchio, arugula, Belgian endive, Romaine hearts, baby spinach, shredded cabbage in a bag. Teddy has a test on salad this week.

"I bet roofers would know how to build a tree house," he says.

Jody smiles at the toddler squirming in his father's arms behind them. The little boy is wearing a toque made to look like a monkey's head, with big eyes goggling on top of his own eyebrows, and the chinstrap consisting of two simian arms, strangling him.

"Why do you want a tree house so badly?" she says.

"I need a man cave. Our place is too small for me to have one inside, so I was thinking I could have one in a tree."

The monkey boy forms his tiny hand into a gun and aims it at Jody. "Pow, pow, pow!" he says. "You're dead! Now I'm going to rape your dead body!"

His father's mouth drops open and he steps out of line with his son, mumbling apologies.

Jody presses herself against Teddy while he pays for their greens.

JODY HAS STILL NOT had an orgasm. She borrowed a book of sex tips from the library a while ago, for ideas on new moves and things. She wanted Teddy to read it with her, but he said why rock the boat when the boat's a-rockin'?

She took things into her own hands and went to a women-centred sex shop. She said she wanted something that would make her feel good, and the multi-pierced clerk held out her small hands to indicate the shelves full of bottles and tubes and ovals and cylinders and pyramids and trapezoids, and told her she needed to be more specific.

Then at Jody's yearly physical, two weeks ago, her family doctor asked if she had any specific complaints, and Jody took a deep breath to steel herself to ask what was normal, in terms of what a normal woman should expect to experience during, say, an average session of common intercourse?

In the quiet examination room, the air whistled and squeaked through Jody's nostrils, and Jody's doctor said, "Ooh, let me take a look in there." She peered up Jody's nose with a tiny bright light and announced, "You have a small polyp on the right side."

"Oh my God." Jody shivered in her paper gown, and the unasked orgasm question flew out of her head and down the hall. "Is it cancer?"

"No, no, not cancer. A nasal polyp is just a fleshy swelling on your sinus lining. It can interfere with things, that's all."

Her doctor sent a referral to an Ear, Nose, and Throat specialist, who would be contacting Jody with an appointment any day now.

JODY WORKS AT THE engraved-metal-plate kiosk in the mall, and Teddy wants her to engrave a bunch of stuff for his parents' anniversary party, mostly because he saw the engraved metal plate on the metal-plate display case that reads, "Adding a metal plate to any gift adds personality."

"Like what kind of stuff?" she says.

They're making love to "Moonlight Desires" by Gowan again, and Teddy says, "Damn, this is a good song," between thrusts. "I thought maybe a trophy."

"A trophy would be nice."

"A Criminal Mind" comes on next, and Jody thinks of rough hands slapping down shingles, ladders slapped up against the side of their house.

"Are you feeling it?" says Teddy.

She is experiencing a low thrumming somewhere she can't quite place. "I'm not sure."

"But it feels good, right?"

She looks past his bare shoulders at their bare walls. They have lived in this apartment for three years and they still haven't decorated.

Teddy's mother says it's because Jody is scared to put down roots.

"Why would I be scared of that?" Jody asked her.

"You tell me," said his mother.

JODY STARES AT HER face in the brass doorknob, far away and then close-up and bulging. When she reaches for herself, the hand coming toward her that is her hand but looks like a monster hand gets bigger and bigger until it eclipses her small form. She takes the monster hand away and there she is again, tiny and alone on the toilet.

She can hear Teddy moving around downstairs. He says he wants her to keep the door open when she's in there. He wants her to feel free and easy with her body. He says maybe that will help things in the "Big O" department, if she knows what he means. But it gets in the way of the sexiness, she tells him. That stuff gets in the way. And Teddy says, "Not in a million years."

There is a scraping sound at the window, and Jody looks over. Roofers. She can make out a bulky form through the gauzy bathroom curtain, and wonders what he can make out from the other side.

Jody finishes and flushes and closes the lid because it's good feng shui. She washes her hands and dries them and goes downstairs.

Teddy is wrapping a present for his parents. The present is a mystery to Jody. He bought it without her, and when he brought the medium-sized bag home, he said, "I want you to be surprised right along with them."

TEDDY'S PLAN IS TO work in a high-end restaurant after college, and then get a TV show.

There is a glut of celebrity chefs, which he is aware of, but he says there's always room for one more, especially one with a gimmick. Teddy hasn't thought of his gimmick yet, but he knows it's out there, waiting for him.

"Maybe I'll only cook easy things," he says. "But with flair. Like I mean my own special flair that no one else can imitate. Or maybe I'll have performing animals on my show. Like dogs and cats rolling around on colourful balls, that sort of thing. And I'll toss them the scraps after I'm done cooking." He shrugs. "It'll come to me."

Jody is jealous of his confidence. She figures you can choose to be inspired when someone is better at something than you are — you can rise to the occasion and do your very best. Or you can let it cripple you. You can give up because it's probably not even worth trying anyway because someone has already done it better than you ever can. Sometimes she gets bursts of crea-tivity at her job, and in addition to the personalized saying on the customer's metal plate, she will add curlicues or other decorative flourishes. But that's about it for inspiration.

Before Jody started working at the metal-plate kiosk, she was with a temp agency.

They found her pretty steady occasional work, in offices mostly, but also in stadiums selling concessions, things like that. Jody's big mistake was when she asked one of her office-job managers if they wanted to just pay her the money they were paying the agency. She felt that showed initiative and forward thinking on her part, but the manager told her agency, and the agency called Jody in for what they called a "closed-door meeting," in which they asked her to stand in the middle of the room and they all sat on chairs in a semi-circle around her and said things like, "You went behind our back, Jody." And, "You violated our code, Jody." And, "After all we've done for you, this is how you repay us." They made her promise never to do that again with one of their clients — because that was the operative thing to remember here; the clients were theirs. And Jody said no, of course not, she would never.

A week later, Jody was shopping at the mall and saw the Help Wanted sign at the metal-plate kiosk, and she jumped at it.

JODY AND TEDDY STAND across the street from their house, watching the roofers toss debris onto their front yard.

Jody pulls a Kleenex out of her coat pocket. "They're not wearing harnesses or anything."

Teddy squints up at the men crouched on the highest peak, hammering. "They're probably wearing harnesses."

"I don't see any." She blows her nose. "This fucking polyp."

"Jody, whoa!"

"There must be ice up there too. They're like daredevils." Jody gazes at the tool belts and the construction boots and says to Teddy, as a joke, "Maybe a roofer will slip me roofies."

Teddy says, "That would not be cool."

She clenches the damp Kleenex in her fist. "Would you kill him?"

He frowns. "We're just talking hypothetically here, right?"

"Can we go in now?" Jody shouts across the street.

The roofer on the ground yells up to the roofers on the roof, "All clear?" And one of them yells back, "All clear!" Then the roofer on the ground tips his hard hat at Jody. "You're all right."

They go inside, and when Teddy heads to the kitchen, Jody goes to her computer and types, "What does an orgasm feel like?" into Google, because maybe she's had one already and she just didn't know it at the time. The first phrase at the top of the search-results page is "a rhythmic thumping."

The phone rings, and it's the Ear, Nose, and Throat specialist's secretary telling her they've booked her in for next Tuesday.

WHEN JODY FIRST MET Teddy, he was in a Gowan cover band. (We're The) Strange Animals played for beers in dark bars, and Jody would stand in the empty space in front of the stage and twirl around.

Teddy was the drummer, which she thought was sexy. She liked being a groupie for her drummer-boyfriend's band. "You guys are really good," she would always say, even though they weren't, because she wanted to have sex with him.

After a while, things got serious, and late at night when they got home from gigs, he would make her dinner.

"This is really good," she would always say, even if it wasn't, because she loved him.

WHEN JODY GETS HOME from work, Teddy's mother is helping Teddy study for his salad exam. The two of them are sitting at the kitchen table with their plates piled with different leaves.

His mother holds up the radicchio. "What's this?"

"I can't remember."

"How about this?" The arugula.

He shakes his head, and pitches an empty spinach clamshell across the room. "I don't know!"

"You have to know," says his mother. "This is part of your Action Plan."

Teddy's mother is a freelance consultant whose specialty, according to her website, is formulating Action Plans. Her website also states, superimposed over a stock photo of blurry seagulls flying over a tranquil beach, that "A career *in* motion is a career with *e*motion."

"You have to use capitals," Teddy has told Jody, "when you talk about your Action Plan. It gives it the necessary oomph." She likes to watch Teddy say "oomph." His lips slide around the word before letting it go.

Teddy's mother says, "You'll have to get on *Restaurant Makeover*."

Teddy nods. "Yeah, that's a good show."

"He has to get a restaurant first," says Jody.

Teddy and his mother look over at her for the first time.

"Don't be so negative, Jody," says his mother. "We're blue-skying here. There is no room in blue-skying for negativity. Oh, and your plants were looking dry, Dear, so I took care of them for you."

Jody immediately goes to the plant they keep in the kitchen and plunges her thumb into the soil, which is soaking wet.

Jody and Teddy have one plant that she wishes they could get rid of, but they can't because it was a gift. His parents gave it to them when they first moved in together, and they've been carting it around to all of their apartments since then. The plant is spindly and looks like it will snap in half if it bends over any farther. It is the type of plant that would whine if it had a voice. Teddy calls it their love plant.

IN BED THE NEXT morning, Teddy says to Jody, "Maybe we should get engaged before my parents' party, what do you think?"

She rolls away from him a little. "What were you and your mother talking about last night?"

"Nothing," he says. "Lettuce."

There is movement at the window, and Jody shushes him.

"I was just thinking it would be nice to introduce you to everybody as my fiancée instead of my girlfriend," he murmurs.

Bang! "So how'd your date go last night, stud?"

Bang! Bang! "Oh yeah, real good. I said to her, 'I want to do you in every hole. I'm talking front door, back door, fucking side door.'"

Teddy whispers to Jody, "What's the side door?"

"I don't know," she whispers back.

THAT NIGHT, JODY HAS a dream about a special door. She is crawling across the room to it on her hands and knees. She tells Teddy, in the dream, that this is going to be the one thing she does today. Her Action Plan is to crawl over to that door and when she gets to it, she'll say, "That's it, that's all for today."

The polyp is in her dream too, but it's a personified polyp, with its own ears, nose, and throat, and eyes. It is looking down at her from the ceiling, telling her that all of her worst fears will come true.

Teddy is making her tea, which he never does in real life. "There is room in here for both of us," he says when the water starts to boil, and he gets down on his hands and knees beside her while the kettle whistles.

"No," says Jody. "This is my thing."

Teddy says, "But I want to help."

"You're not helping," she tells him, and changes her crawl to a wiggle. "If you don't get up now, the kettle will run dry and burn on the bottom."

He tries to tell her about his day. "I was hungry and I only had one arm because I chopped off the other one in class, so I figured, something easy. Something I wouldn't have to peel or scoop."

Jody is not even a quarter of the way across the room. She has barely moved.

"I went to buy a slice of pizza but the crust was too thick at the place in the mall. I thought, 'There's not enough choice in this food court.'"

She bares her teeth and her neck tendons jump. She thinks, *There is a real me who is itching to get out. I am in this cocoon and I want to emerge.*

Teddy says, "I said to myself, 'Maybe a plain bun. But then where's the protein?'"

JODY TYPES, "CONGRATULATIONS CONRAD and Shirley! 43 years and still going strong!" into the computerized engraver and hits the start button.

She likes the feel of a metal plate's hard edges in her hand. It feels official. When the machine spits out the tester plate, she holds the shiny rectangle up to her eyes and winks at her reflection.

The little radio she keeps by the cash starts playing Gowan's "(You're A) Strange Animal," which used to be Jody's favourite cover tune because Teddy had a drum solo in his band's version. She hums along and twirls around the kiosk, alone in the empty mall.

They'll embellish the whole thing later, like how he got down on one knee, or concealed the ring in a piece of cake. Something like that. They'll make it a more romantic story when they tell people. People only care about the story, anyway.

WHEN JODY GETS HOME, there is an ambulance in front of her house, and police cars.

A bunch of her neighbours are standing around, or at least people she assumes are her neighbours, some of them with winter coats on and some of them without. They are all rubbing their arms and shaking their heads and blowing out white plumes of frozen breath that remind Jody of the smoke machine that used to transform Teddy's band into something bigger and better than it was.

Jody starts to walk toward the yellow police tape stretched

across the short pathway to her door, but a woman wearing a parka over bare legs and slippers grabs her elbow.

"You can't go in there," the woman says, with some authority. "It's a crime scene."

"It's my apartment," says Jody. "I live there."

An excited murmuring rises from the crowd along with the fluffy white exhalations.

The front yard is a mess. The snow is littered with more roofing debris than usual, and numerous emergency personnel are waving their arms and shaking their heads and slamming doors on their various emergency vehicles.

"An accident," someone says. "A horrible accident."

Jody takes a few steps back. She will have to be the messenger. She will have to call back everyone on the list and explain to Teddy's parents' friends and relatives and neighbours and former co-workers that there has been an accident. Yes, she'll tell them, it was a horrible accident. So I think you'll agree that it's best if we don't — exactly. You understand, of course. Because they'll be in mourning. May 5th, that's right. Oh, I think they'd still be — yes. So I don't think a celebration would be, no. Not after this. It wouldn't be the same happy occasion. Oh, you're welcome. It's a hard thing, yes. But I'm the one who needs to make these calls, because I was his fiancée. Thank you, that's very kind of you. I'm holding up. Yes, we were planning the wedding, we were going to get married. We hadn't set a date yet, no, we were leaving it open. No, I hadn't bought a dress. But I'd started looking around at a few places. In the mall. We hadn't booked anything yet, no. So that's a small mercy, yes, I suppose you're right.

Then she will have to call his parents. Or she should probably call them first. They would want to know before other people. She can't decide if she should tell them about the party. They would probably be touched that he had thought of them in such a celebratory way. It might be a nice thing to tell them, after the rest of it.

A light goes on in her apartment, in the living room.

Someone says, "The roof. A roofer."

Someone else says, "No harness, what the hell was he thinking?"

And Jody looks up to see Teddy framed in their living-room window, waving at her. Except for his slowly moving arm, he's a perfect cardboard cut-out of himself, all smooth contours and durable design. She can picture him on television.

THE EAR, NOSE, AND THROAT specialist has hair growing out of his ears and nose, and he keeps clearing his throat, alternating between "ems" and "hehms". Jody reclines in his big chair while he reads the health questionnaire she filled out in the waiting room.

He puts down her chart and sits on a wheeled stool. He wheels himself up close, the hem of his white coat flapping a little in the breeze this motion makes. He looks inside her ears with a scope, and peers up her nostrils with a tiny bright light. He tells her to open wide and say, "Ahh," and depresses her tongue with a fat popsicle stick and examines her throat.

"Do you have to do it in that order?" she asks him.

He points the popsicle stick at her. "Your nose is always blocked or dripping, and you have trouble breathing. These symptoms are very common."

"They are?"

He nods. "They're being caused by a small, right-sided nasal polyp."

"That polyp is ruining my life," she says.

"I can remove it," he tells her. "I have all the tools. I can do a polypectomy right here in the office."

"Right here?" says Jody. "On this chair?"

"I'll need to freeze you first. After that, the procedure is a very simple one." He turns away from her to assemble some equipment on the side table. "Is there someone to take care of you?"

She sits up straighter. "I have a fiancé."

"That's good. You might be a bit woozy afterwards, so it helps to have someone to bring you home."

"Oh, he's not here." She slumps. "He's at chef school."

"Well, as long as you're not driving."

"I'm not."

"Good." The specialist turns back around and smiles at her. "And you'll have a husband who can cook, lucky you. Now, just relax." He takes her chin in his hand and tilts her head back. Then he holds what looks like a set of blunt pliers up to her face, and she flinches. "You're all right," he says, and his breath is warm on her face.

Jody lies there while the specialist pries open each of her nostrils with the pliers, and uses a silver can with a long nozzle to spray inside. Then he pats his knees and stands up. "Now we just have to wait for the freezing to take effect."

He leaves her alone in the room, going numb. The bitter anesthetic drips down the back of her throat, and she winces. When she swallows, it's like a hand is wrapped around her neck, squeezing slowly. She closes her eyes and sees Teddy wearing the black leather gloves he used to wear on stage. She asked him to wear them to bed once and he did, but when she said, "I want you to pretend to strangle me," he took them off, and frowned at her.

When the specialist comes back, he is carrying a gleaming metal instrument with a long, thin rod at one end. "I'm going to insert this into your right nasal passageway," he says, "to suction and debride your polyp so it won't bother you anymore."

"Thank God," she says, and then, "Will it hurt?"

"No, not at all. You are completely frozen."

"Okay." She leans back, uncurling herself against the smooth blue vinyl of the specialist's chair. "I'm ready."

He uses the pliers again, and then slips the rod into her widened right nostril. "Here we go," he says, and he's right. She doesn't feel a thing.

The Healing Arts

ON MY WAY HOME from work the other day, I was waiting for the streetcar and I became mesmerized by a photocopied poster stuck to a cement pole. It had a photo of a guy's fist clenched around a bunch of bills, and it said, TIRED OF MAKING SOMEBODY ELSE RICH? TIRED OF THE RAT RACE? TIRED OF BEING SICK AND TIRED?

I thought to myself, *Yeah, you know what? I am*. And I could tell everybody around me was looking at this poster too and probably thinking the same thing. My fellow rats.

MICHAEL SAYS THAT HAVING a dream is a humbling experience because you might very well never achieve it.

My dream is not something I have shared with a lot of people because it's pretty private. Although the fact is that if you want your dream to come true, you have to not be afraid to tell other people about it, so those other people can help you in your dream-achieving quest. Then of course there is always the slight risk that one of those people will steal your dream, but you can't let that stop you from publicizing your innermost greatest wishes, or else you're right back where you started and you have made no progress at all.

Sometimes I feel like I'm not where I should be, and I worry about the progress, or should I say lack of progress, I have made thus far. Because although I own a home and have a wife, which are certainly milestones, I have not yet achieved my dream.

Michael says I shouldn't worry about what I'm doing with my life. He says you never want to set your bar too high because then it might trip you. He says lives are for living, and that's why we're going to the Auto Show.

MICHAEL'S DREAM IS TO be a photographer, and he's already well on his way to full, or at least partial, realization. He photographed his sister's wedding last fall, and almost all of his pictures were way better than the ones she got from the asshole she hired.

Michael also does this very enterprising thing where he stands around Nathan Phillips Square and takes snapshots of tourists against picturesque Toronto backgrounds like the Eaton Centre and the TD Bank. Then he gives the tourists his email address so they can get in touch if they want to purchase their one-of-a-kind souvenir photo.

Sometimes I feel myself getting slightly jealous over his forward momentum, but I would never let that get in the way of our friendship. Michael is my best friend, which is why I'm the guy going with him to see a collection of some of the most deluxe vehicles in the world.

We meet up with Michael's ex, Darlene, outside the convention centre in the morning to get our tickets. She's wearing an ID badge with her photo on it.

Michael leans in and frowns at her picture. "Who took that?"

She shrugs. "I don't know. The ID badge photographer. There were a bunch of them."

He shakes his head. "It's a terrible shot of you."

"Gee, thanks."

Darlene is obviously a bitch because she's Michael's ex. But she was at least nice enough to get us complimentary Friends & Family tickets. She's a shammy girl for Toyota so she has special privileges like that.

We haven't told her that we have an ulterior motive underlying our desire to attend the Auto Show, which is that Michael is going to take the most amazing car photos ever, and then auction them off online to the highest bidders.

In her spare time, Darlene makes see-through soaps with little plastic animals inside. She gave Michael a ton of them before they broke up, and he told me they're still the only soap he uses, even though after a few washes, the sharp bits of the animals stick out and scrape him.

"You should really go back and get that re-taken," Michael tells her.

Darlene hands him our tickets. "You're hilarious."

"Why do you always say that, Darlene?"

She pats him on the cheek. "You just are."

MY DREAM IS — DEEP breath here! — to practise the Healing Arts.

It all started when I was very young, and my parents took me to see a children's performer at the Phil and Sondra LaFoy Memorial Auditorium, which my mother told me was named after a couple who loved each other so much that they died on the exact same day, and then their family went and paid to put their names on a heart-shaped plaque to make everybody else feel bad about their own love.

The performer wasn't very good, probably that's why his show was free, but the other kids seemed to like him. Halfway through a trick that involved a stuffed dog (I remember thinking to myself at the time, *He can't even use a real dog? You can find a dog anywhere!*), he got a weird look on his face, as if he'd forgotten something important at home, and then he fell over, right there on stage.

At first the audience thought it was part of the act, and they laughed. But gradually, as the performer lay there doing nothing, and the stuffed dog with its rolling googly eyes lay pitifully on the stage beside him, there was some muttering in the crowd. Then a few people started screaming.

My parents tell me (and I have my own vague recollection of this) that I walked up the aisle to the stage in a very deliberate way, and I climbed up and sat down next to the unmoving man.

There were a few scattered cries of, "Get that kid out of there!" and "Keep that kid away from him, he might have injured his spine!"

But then the expressed worry and outrage gave way to an awed silence when I rolled up my sleeves and placed my hands on the fallen performer's neck and chest. I closed my eyes and commenced to rock back and forth, and hum.

Then the performer let out a loud groan, and everyone seemed to inhale all at once, at which point the performer sat up and blinked and looked around. And then — this is my favourite part — the entire audience spontaneously broke into enthusiastic applause. For me.

Did the performer have a heart attack and die? Did I bring him back to life with my gift of the Healing Arts? We will never truly know. But I think so.

THEN YOU HAVE MY wife Josefina, who when I met her, I just knew. Like they say you're supposed to know.

Mutual friends introduced us at a party. First, they said to me, "There's this woman you have to meet." I nodded at Josefina across the room. "Do you mean that woman over there?" They said, "Oh, you two are already acquainted, then?" "No," I said. "I just knew that's who you were talking about."

We think alike. For example, we have this antique plate that her mother gave us the first time we told her and Josefina's father that Josefina was pregnant. The plate is cracked right up the middle, but we keep using it because we want to see how long it will last and how much stuff we can put on it before it breaks into a million pieces.

THE BOOTH BABE IN the Cadillac Zone has veins popping out all over her body, which is mostly uncovered, naturally, since she's a booth babe. Her veins are like my mother-in-law's veins, which according to the doctors is because her blood is dangerously close to the surface.

Michael says, "Do you want to hear a universal truth, Deano?"

I say, "I sure do."

"The plusher the car, the plusher the carpet." He nods down at his feet. "Look at this stuff — you sink right in. You can barely see my shoes."

I wiggle my own feet on the soft floor and marvel at the plushness.

Michael aims his camera at the Escalade next to the booth babe. "Ideally, you want to get the babe, the car, and the sign that says what kind of car it is." He takes a picture and then looks at it in the viewfinder, frowning a little. Then he snaps another one, because he's a perfectionist.

Michael says his favourite thing about being a photographer is he has the power to make people smile. Here you are, pointing this little black box at somebody and you press a button and you're even stealing their soul, according to some primitive cultures, and your subject smiles and smiles until you tell them to stop.

When we walk away, Michael says to me, "Deano, do you ever say something, like out loud, and to your own ears your voice doesn't sound like your voice at all? It sounds like somebody else's voice?"

"I don't think so," I say.

"It's fucking spooky, man." Michael shakes his head. "Let's go get some pizza."

ALL OF MY AND Josefina's immediate neighbours are getting AstroTurf lawns, and they're bugging me to go in with them because they're getting a group deal, and apparently one more person will substantially sweeten the discount. But I said no way.

I know it would be more convenient and it would be green all the time, even in the winter. Michael says I'm an idiot, and he would do it if he was me, because who wants to rake? Who wants to fertilize?

The thing is, you've got all these environmental types being so in-your-face these days, like the professional midgets they hired at the Auto Show to run around in loincloths and leaf necklaces telling everybody to consider buying a hybrid this year. Which is demeaning, no question, but they still pissed me off.

It all adds up and gets to be too much, and sometimes I want to seriously shit all over the planet. Like eat out of Styrofoam containers all day with plastic cutlery, and put all my leftovers in Ziplock bags, and for fruit I would eat only Fruit Roll-ups, that sort of thing. And I would only buy products that were individually wrapped in non-recyclable plastic packaging, like a #6, and the packaging itself would be shrink-wrapped.

But then I rein myself in by thinking that we have to preserve this world for our children, or at the very least our children's children. Or other people's children, whatever. The point is, I'm not getting the AstroTurf.

SOME ASSHOLE AT THE Auto Show is taking people's pictures in front of a green screen, and Michael says he wants to get an eyeball at the software he's using. Then he can procure the same program, download it or whatever, and go out and do exactly the same thing that this asshole's doing, except better, so he can charge more.

Michael says it's guys like this who are ruining it for the rest of us. And if you ask me, I think he's right. So what, this asshole buys himself a green screen, a couple of lights, then buys the software that really does all the work for him, oh yeah and an expensive camera, and then he's out there doing it. He makes it look so easy but Michael says that when something looks easy, that just means there's a trick involved. Somebody is always getting tricked when somebody else is doing something so-called special. Michael says everybody deserves a chance to live their dream, and it's not fair for only a select few to get all the glory, and through trickery especially.

He says he heard somewhere that a person has to put in so many hours at something to get good at it, as in to be considered a professional in the field and to start receiving acclaim. Michael is putting in his hours, no doubt about it, but he also says whatever happened to natural talents and abilities? I tell him that's what I would like to know.

MY WIFE JOSEFINA'S DREAM is to be a mother. In this quest, she has been doing a lot of soul-searching lately, which I find admirable. I said to her the other day, "Josefina, you are amazingly introspective." And she said, "What's that supposed to mean?"

What I meant is just that I'm not like that, but I wish I could be. I wish I could have a bird's-eye view of my mind and my emotional insides like my wife does about herself.

She went through a phase a little while ago where she cut all the tags out of her clothes, the ones that tell you the size and the washing instructions. She said she had come to the realization that she could do that, and that she would be more comfortable that way. She didn't need to consult a label to figure out how to wash a shirt from Old Navy.

Josefina also likes to set the timer on the microwave to random amounts of time — minutes, seconds — and see how much she can accomplish before it beeps. Sometimes she gets a lot done. Other times she marvels that fifty-five seconds one day feels so much shorter than fifty-five seconds last week.

MICHAEL IS A GENEROUS guy. If he sees an old lady, for instance, who is in dire need of some sort of assistance, he will be the first to offer it. He will step up to the plate and do whatever it is that this old lady needs. He cares about the lesser people, the ones who don't have advantages like him and me. Not that we were born with a silver spoon or anything, but you know, we would never walk on the little people for our own personal gain.

Not like this asshole with the green screen.

That's why guys like him burn us up so bad. He's got all this fancy equipment and yet he probably pays his workers next to nothing. And everyone is all, "Oh, you're so smart, Mr. Photographer Man!"

Michael, who has had to scrape and claw to get to where he is today, has a true appreciation for the hardship involved in building his own business. He is an artisan. Myself, I want to be a Healing Artisan, but I have a lot further to go in my personal path, compared to where Michael is on his journey.

But this photographer — he is an asshole.

WHEN I WAS IN high school, my mother was very overweight, and I was embarrassed to be seen with her. One day I got so fed up with being seen with such a fat, ugly mother, that I rolled up my sleeves and laid my hands on her fat stomach when she was snacking on a Flakey in our kitchen.

I started rocking back and forth and humming, and she dropped the Flakey in surprise, or else because she was overcome by all the healing going on. But in any case, the Flakey was on the floor and no longer going into her mouth, and she started to cry.

My mother lost about twenty pounds over the next few months or so, and then she went to the mall and headed straight for one of those makeover kiosks and bought herself a make-over. Then she was beautiful like I remembered her being when I was little, and I didn't mind when she drove me to school or accompanied me and my father to my graduation ceremony.

Was it a healing miracle that I performed, or simply a happy coincidence? You tell me.

JOSEFINA THINKS THE WORLD is out to get her sometimes. She has this book that she hates, it's a stir-fry cookbook and she says none of the recipes have ever turned out right. The book is called *Jimmy Wong's Stir Fry Bible*, and Josefina says it's a pack of lies. She has never, via Jimmy Wong's instructions, made her baby corns and pea shoots taste like they do at a Chinese restaurant. She says just seeing this book on our bookshelf makes her feel like jumping off a bridge.

One day I told her, "What you should do is, you should take it to the library. The library can always use more books, right?" So that's what she did. She went and dumped it in the return slot with a few other actual library books that were overdue.

The next week she was at the counter checking out some

magazines, and the librarian scanned her card and suddenly got all excited. He said, "Wait right here — I have something for you!" Josefina counted out her change for the late fee, and when the librarian came back, he smacked old Jimmy Wong down on the counter triumphantly and said, "I believe this is yours." The only explanation we could figure is the library books she dumped in with Jimmy were the only other books in there, so they correctly assumed that *Jimmy Wong's Stir Fry Bible* belonged to her as well.

She brought the book back home, in tears. I said to her, "Babe, leave it on the curb and somebody will pick it up. Everybody likes a good stir fry." To which she gave me a bit of a look, which I deserved. Then she put Jimmy back on our shelf and said it would be a reminder to her that none of her wishes in life would ever come true. Which I thought was a little crazy, but I wasn't going to tell her that.

MICHAEL IS TRYING TO see what kind of software the green-screen photographer is using.

We're standing behind the velvet rope — of course this asshole uses a velvet rope — and Michael is leaning over it to squint at the photo assistant's computer screen, which is next to a large plastic container of Mothers Against Drunk Driving mints.

The assistant turns around. She's wearing a tuxedo shirt with a bow tie even though she's not a man, and her long hair is pulled back from her face, stretching her skin too tight. "Can I help you?" She points to the container. "Would you like to donate fifty cents to MADD? You get a mint if you want. It's the peppermint-patty kind, they're chocolate-enrobed."

Michael winks and says, "I do this." He wiggles his camera at her.

"That's nice." The assistant smiles a not-very-nice smile, and does up the top button on her shirt.

"So where can I buy this set-up?"

She scowls at him, and waves to the photographer.

The photographer ambles over with a big fake grin yanking up the corners of his stupid mouth. "Can I help you?"

"Yeah," says Michael, "I was wondering where I can purchase this green-screen set-up for myself. Being as I am a fellow shutterbug and all." He holds up his camera again.

The photographer drops his grin. "There are a bunch of different components."

"Okay, yeah, I get that. So where can I buy the components?"

"Different places." The photographer wiggles his own camera, which is bigger than Michael's. "Would you gentlemen like to get your picture taken today?"

"Yeah, what the hell," says Michael, and starts to duck under the velvet rope.

The photographer nods at the long lineup winding around the Jeep Wrangler on the other side of the green screen. "Sorry, guys, you have to line up over there." He doesn't sound sorry at all.

Michael doesn't move, and neither do I. The crowd noises sort of die around us, and I hear the pre-recorded Auto Show announcer's voice clearer than I've heard it before. He's telling us we can win a trip for two to Hawaii if we enter the draw in the Ferrari area, and I make a mental note to do that because who doesn't want a trip to Hawaii?

Michael says, "Okay, so how about if I want to buy a Jeep? Are you going to stand there and not tell me where I can find one of those too?"

"I don't sell cars." The photographer stands a little straighter. "I take pictures. Jeep is my client."

"Your client."

"What was that?"

"Nothing. Let's go, Deano." Michael jerks his head at me, and I follow him to the back of the line.

When it's our turn, we get to choose the background for our photo. Michael tells me to pick because that's the kind of guy he is, he's magnanimous. All of the backgrounds have some sort of animal and some sort of vegetation in them.

"The theme is Getting Back To Nature," says the prop girl, who's dressed in a green bikini with a rubber snake draped over her shoulders. "Like how the Jeep Wrangler can take you effortlessly into the forest or even the jungle, you know. Anywhere with plants."

I decide on the one that has a meadow with a bunch of dopey-looking sheep standing around, because it's funny. The prop girl gives me a giant shepherd's crook to hold for authenticity.

AT ONE POINT, JOSEFINA'S parents mailed us a card with a cartoon lamb on it. Later on, Josefina wanted to throw the card away, but I kept it without telling her. I put it in a drawer. Sometimes I pull it out and look at the lamb when she's not around, and it makes me smile.

The lamb is the happiest creature I've ever seen. The background is bright pink and so are the flowers and the grass under its little hooves, as if light from the lamb's very heart is shining out its various holes.

If we could all be this way, so carefree and with a bell on a ribbon around our soft necks, ringing out our intentions and our best memories of ourselves that we share in the hopes of becoming more intimate with our loved ones, then the world would benefit in untold measurements. Because we're all so busy worrying about what's going to happen next, we forget to experience the moment at hand. Even though something horrible might be lurking right around the corner, this lamb is clearly embracing the here and now.

MICHAEL WILL SAY TO me, "Deano, no one is going to bend their ass backwards to give you a fucking break in this life, so you have to make your own breaks and cut your own slack."

Josefina is my break. She dazzles me. Even though she might not be aware of this herself. The things she has put herself through, and it's all been for us. And I am not aware of a single thing I can do to make her realize her own worth.

She says she always thought she existed to bring a new person into the world, and if she can't even do that, then what good is she? I say, "We can keep on being this great team, Josefina. Hey, we're like kids already, the two of us against the big bad world and so on. Instead of getting crushed by the weight of the world's problems and our own, we can treat it all like one big play-ground, right?" But then she goes all superstitious on me. She says when we're apart, she pictures all sorts of ugly things hap-pening to me. I say, "Baby, you can't worry all the time like that. It's not healthy. Turn off the news if it helps. Don't read the headlines." She loves 680 News. I don't get it. It's all bad news all the time, shouting in your ears while you're trying to enjoy a nice drive. And we don't even own a car.

Josefina thinks if you get your hopes up about something, you'll ruin it. I tell her that's negative thinking, which will get you precisely nowhere in this life. We got past the three-month mark with the last one, and we celebrated with a little cake. She said, "How about only a cupcake?" And I said, "No, let's have a real, actual cake, but just make it small."

MICHAEL AND I GO back to the Pizza Pizza booth for dinner because there's something special about how they do their pizza at the Auto Show. All of the slices are arranged separately on silver shelves, and they have a crispness around the edges that they don't have normally.

Michael chews and says to me, "You know what we should do? We should wipe that smirk off that asshole's face. Just erase it completely."

"Oh, yeah?" I say.

Then Darlene comes over in her uniform, which is a tank top and shorts cut to look like two tires. Her dirty shammy cloth is hanging from her belt like a dead thing. "You guys are still here?"

Michael says, "How's the rub-and-tug business going? Get it? Because you're rubbing cars and, you know, tugging on your cleaning rag?"

"You're hilarious." She puts a hand on my shoulder and squeezes gently. "How's Josefina doing?"

"She's good," I say. "She's taking some time off work."

"I could do with some of that." With her free hand, she grabs her shammy and shakes it over her head like a pom-pom.

"Hey, Darlene," says Michael, "what time does everybody pack up around here?"

"After all the bozos like you go home."

"Where are you parked?"

"The staff parking lot in the basement. If you think I'm driving you, you are sorely mistaken."

Michael looks at her hand on my shoulder. "I still use your animals."

"Good for you."

MICHAEL SAYS PEOPLE LIKE to believe they are emotionally prepared for their lives, but speaking in generalities, this is almost never the case. He says the way it goes is, your life goes one way and you're all like, *Okay, whoa, hold on, what happened? I didn't actually make that decision right there. That decision was made for me.*

Okay, so you're a kid, right? You're playing the game where you walk home through the ditches in the long grass pretending like you're on an African safari, with a gun that is actually a stick. A fun little kid's game. You may even be singing a song you made up on the spot because you were a creative kid that way, before you ever even started taking pictures. Or healing people, as is the case with me.

And then bang, here you are in this job you're not too keen on, working with these people who are not too keen on you. And then your wife gets pregnant, and sure, you had something to do with that, but you didn't really think the whole thing through. Then she loses the baby, but it's okay because it's not actually a baby at that point, like she told you. So you think, *Well, I guess I dodged the bullet there.* Kind of a sad situation, but hey, you would have had zero chance of quitting your crappy job if that kid decided to stick around and went on to sing songs and tramp through ditches on its way home.

So you go to work after all that's said and done and you still don't give your notice, but you're a little bit closer to that day.

IT'S KIND OF POETIC that we're hanging around in a parking lot after the Auto Show. I voice something along those lines to Michael and he says, "Yeah, whatever." When I ask him what we're waiting for, he doesn't say anything. He places his camera on the hood of somebody's car, and crosses his arms.

Something clicks in my brain, and I remember about the Hawaii contest, which I forgot to enter. We even went by the Ferrari area so Michael could take a picture, but the contest totally slipped my mind. I picture Josefina and me on a white-sand beach with a couple of big umbrella drinks. I say, "Michael, we have to go back inside."

"Shut up, Deano."

Then I see the asshole with the green screen and his assistant, pushing their equipment out the doors. They're chatting away, all friendly, and I wonder if maybe he's paying her a decent wage after all. She seems happy enough to be working for him. And he didn't make her dress up like a slut, which has to count for something.

Michael yells, "Deano, grab the girl!" and the next thing I know, I'm stepping forward and I've got my arms around this young woman and she's screaming and kicking and whipping her ponytail in my face, so I let her go, and Michael swears at me while he punches the photographer, and the assistant is crying and running away, and yelling in a high-pitched voice that hurts my ears, "I'm calling 911, I'm calling 911!"

Michael is kicking the photographer in the legs and the stomach and the head. The guy is grunting, down on his knees and then flat on his back, and there's blood and Michael's shoes are flying and stomping and he calls to me, "Deano, get over here!"

So I do, and when I'm closer I can see there's not much left of the photographer's face, it's a big mess. I taste the pizza on its way back up, and it's not so delicious now. I puke next to the guy but try really hard to aim away from his head because there's not much he can do to shield himself.

"Hold him!" Michael yells.

I say, "But he's not moving."

The photographer's bags and bins have spilled onto the pavement, and the cart he was using to move everything is upended with one of its wheels spinning in the air. The fluorescent lights glint off a pile of silver coins, which it takes me a minute to realize are the foil-wrapped Mothers Against Drunk Driving mints.

Michael goes over to the largest black bag and rummages through it. He lets out a victorious "Hah!" and lifts the photographer's big camera over his head, the strap dangling. He walks back to the man on the ground and stands over him.

"Michael," I say.

Michael holds the camera in front of his face. He points it down at the guy and says, "Smile."

The photographer wheezes out pink bubbles.

Michael sort of comes back into himself, and he shakes his

head like he's trying to clear it. He loops the photographer's camera strap around his neck, and picks his own camera off the car hood. Then he leans over and spits on the guy's face. "All you had to do was share a little bit of information, one professional to another. That's all you had to do." He turns to me. "Let's go." And then, "Deano, are you coming or what?"

Because I'm rolling up my sleeves and kneeling down next to the guy. My hands are twitching, and I want to lay them on this photographer and see what happens. I could rock back and forth and hum and see if he gets back up.

Michael swears at me some more and runs, and I stay put. I prod the photographer's chest with my fingertips and feel a soft sort of dent, like a bruise on an apple. The blood is everywhere and the photographer is moaning in the quietest voice, I can hardly hear him, and he's staring at me with the one eye he can get open, barely.

I look up at the concrete ceiling and wait to feel whatever it is I'm supposed to feel, a tingling or whatever, but there's nothing. I try to concentrate and hone in on the healing magic, but I'm so pathetically out of practice. I hear a siren far off in the distance and I think about how good it would feel to really achieve something, through actual perseverance instead of just the luck of the draw.

I don't even bother rocking back and forth and humming because I can already tell it's not going to work. I don't have the power of the Healing Arts and who knows, I probably never did. I shrug in a basically helpless way at the photographer because that's how I feel. I'm a helpless, useless rat and there's nothing I can do for him.

"My wife is at home," I tell him. "She's waiting for me." I stand up, and he moans again. "I have to go, I'm sorry. The ambulance is coming, though. They'll know what to do."

THE OTHER DAY I was in line buying groceries after work, and I noticed this couple ahead of me. The guy was talking too loudly to the girl, and expressing pure astonishment at everything she was saying, like he was trying to sound more enthusiastic than he felt. He also kept rubbing her back, as if the things he used to like about her would return to him through her skin and T-shirt fabric to his hand.

I watched our milk and eggs and bread inch forward on the conveyor belt and I thought to myself, *Josefina and me, we're better than these people. We don't have to put on a show like that, because we understand each other. The two of us have an understanding.* And I felt better.

Earlier Versions of the Following Stories Were Published Previously:

"Some Wife" appeared in *Matrix*, and was part of *Those Girls*, a chapbook published by Greenboathouse Books.

"What I Would Say" appeared in *THIS Magazine*.

"Our Many-Splendoured Humanity" appeared in *Taddle Creek*.

"The Only One" appeared in *The Antigonish Review*.

"We Are All About Wendy Now" appeared in *Indiana Review*.

"Todd and Belinda Rivers of 780 Strathcona" appeared in Joyland.ca.

"Ear, Nose, and Throat" appeared in *The New Quarterly*.

Thank you to the editors of these magazines. Also thanks to the editors of *Forget Magazine, Geist, Kiss Machine*, and *The Puritan* for publishing stories not included in this collection.

Acknowledgements

FOR CAREFUL AND ENTHUSIASTIC reading, thank you to Suzanne
Andrew, Kate & Lori Barton, Jonathan Bennett, Ryan Bigge,
Eugenia Canas, Jeff Chapman, Peter Darbyshire, Betty Dick, Rob
Elliott, Lorne Hicks, Pasha Malla, Jasmine Macaulay, Don McKellar,
Jim Munroe, Jen Noble, Emily Pohl-Weary, Pauline Rentzelos,
Kevin Robinson, Sandra Ridley, Craig Taylor, Matthew Trafford,
Samantha Warwick, the Wuenschirs family, G'ma W, and Cameron
& Marcella.

Many thanks to Elizabeth Ruth for wisdom; Nathaniel G.
Moore for WWF-strength cheering; the Salonists for brilliance;
Aunt Chris for her poems; and to Andrew, Meg, and Caroline.

Thank you to the great reading series that have kindly hosted
me over the years, especially Stan Rogal & Stephen Humphrey
of the Idler Pub, Bill Kennedy & Angela Rawlings of The Lex,
Paul Vermeersch & Alex Boyd of the I.V. Lounge, Liz Clayton
& Damian Rogers of Pontiac Quarterly, Carey Toane of Pivot,

and Dan Evans at The Bookshelf.

I'm enormously grateful for the funding I've received from the Canada Council for the Arts, and the Ontario Arts Council Writers' Reserve Program (with many thanks to the publishers who recommended me).

I'm indebted to Sarah Henstra, Grace O'Connell, and Sarah Selecky of The Jupiter Group, for dazzling inspiration, support, and story insight.

Thanks to Sam Hiyate, Super Agent, for being in my corner.

Thank you to Marc Côté for his belief in these stories, his guidance, and his deft edits; to Carolyn McNeillie for her keen-eyed copy edit; to Barry Jowett for his meticulous proofread; to Meryl Howsam for publicity magic; to Angel Guerra and Tannice Goddard for their lovely design work; and to everyone else at Cormorant Books.

Many thanks to Lindsay Page for her beautiful cover art, which fills me with delight each time I see it.

My deepest love and gratitude are saved for Derek Wuenschirs, champion Foto Hunter and the best ever, for making me laugh every day.

About the Author

JESSICA WESTHEAD'S SHORT STORIES have appeared in major literary journals in Canada and the United States. "Unique and Life-Changing Items," which appears in this collection, was short-listed for the CBC Literary Awards. Her first novel, *Pulpy & Midge*, was nominated for the ReLit Award. Westhead lives in Toronto.